CEMENT STILETTOS

SAMANTHA KIDD STYLE & ERROR MYSTERY #7

DIANE VALLERE

Polyester Press

CEMENT STILETTOS

Book 7 in the Samantha Kidd Style & Error Mystery Series

A Polyester Press Publication

This is a work of fiction. Characters, places, and events are the product of the author's imagination or are used fictitiously. Any resemblance to real people, companies, institutions, organizations, or incidents is entirely coincidental.

ebook edition

First published June 2017

Print ISBN: 9781939197320

DIANE VALLERE'S WEEKLY DIVA!

A Weekly DiVa Exclusive!

Sign up to receive The Weekly DiVa and get the first book I ever wrote (in high school!*) + packing tips! Because I am multi-talented.

*it was the 80s. Adjust your reading expectations as necessary.

To Bruno's Pizza

SAMANTHA 2.0

*F*or the record, it was seven days after I slipped on the engagement ring when Nick and I got into our first argument. Any judge in the country would have agreed it was all his fault.

"No," he said.

"'No?' Just— 'no'? You're saying no to me just like that?" I slammed my coffee cup on my kitchen counter a little too hard and hot liquid splashed out onto my thumb. I shook the droplets off and blotted the spill with a paper towel.

"That's right. I'm saying no, just like that. I mean it, Kidd. Don't fight me on this."

"But it's my life and I can do whatever I want with it. And just because we're getting married—someday—doesn't mean you can tell me what to do."

Logan, my black cat and second in command in Chez Kidd, slunk into the kitchen and buried his head in his bowl. He'd been slightly less vocal about supporting me since I put him on a diet a few months ago, but still, I'd hoped for a hiss or a growl to let Nick know it was two against one.

"I'm not telling you what to do," Nick said. "I'm telling you what you're not going to do. You're not spending the last day of your first vacation in two years traipsing around run-down factories in a sketchy part of town with me."

"Why not? Like you said, it's my last day of vacation. I should be able to spend it how I want. Besides, you're leaving for Italy in a week."

"I would have thought you'd be more interested in going to Italy with me. Italy has pizza."

"Empty factories sound interesting. You never know what you'll find," I said. "Besides, I want to spend more time with you."

"That's sweet, Kidd. It is. But after I gave you forty pair of shoes for Christmas, you forgot I was even in the room. My showroom manager already arranged my schedule for today and it's going to be tight. You'll be a distraction." I crossed my arms over my pajamas. "A good distraction. But why visiting empty factories sounds more interesting to you than milking the last day of your vacation is beyond me."

He may have had a point.

"Fine," I said. "Go conqueror the designer shoe world."

He bent down and kissed me. "I have to get going. Meet me at my showroom tonight? I'll take you out to dinner. But don't show up a minute before six because I do have a lot of work to do."

"Okay." I pretended to pout. He kissed me again and then left.

I cleaned up after a breakfast of toaster waffles and coffee and went to the bedroom. It may seem odd that my first proper vacation in two years was making me antsy. Sure, the first few days came with the luxuries of sleeping in, eating ice cream for breakfast, and helping Logan play with his new catnip toys, but after being employment-challenged for almost two years, the aimless days were starting to feel familiar, and not in a good way. Everybody I knew either had returned to work or had a baby. (One person I knew had a baby, but she'd temporarily moved in with her brother in Philly while her house here in Ribbon was being prepped for sale.)

Nick wasn't being entirely altruistic when he turned down my offer to "help" him. The last time I'd tried to help him at work hadn't ended well. It may have had something to do with me prioritizing a murder investigation over the work he'd expected from me. I liked to think I'd matured a bit since then, but I understood why he wasn't willing to chance it. Nick didn't know I'd kicked off the new year and our engagement with a whole battery of resolutions. I was going to be a better version of myself: more focused, professional, and thoughtful. I was going to become Samantha 2.0.

I showered and changed into a white shirt and black leather leggings and blow dried my hair. I added silver hoop earrings and a silver tank watch, pulled on a navy blue shrunken blazer and ankle booties, kissed Logan between his pointy black ears, and headed to the store where I worked, one day early.

Tradava was a local department store in the process of establishing itself as a reputable, mid-range retailer. Growing up, I remembered the store for its toy department and annual outdoor tent sales of aisles bursting with discount items. As a teen, I'd spent a fair portion of my allowance on accessories like lace gloves, gummy bracelets, and the occasional *Flashdance* sweatshirt. I'd moved away for college and then work in New York City, but two years ago, when I gave up the life I knew, I'd moved back and stumbled into a job working at the store. In my time away, they'd leveraged their roots in the community to build their brand as a family-owned chain with ties to the bigger cities of Philadelphia and New York to the east.

I parked around back of the store in the employee lot. The biting January wind snapped at my cheeks and whipped my hair around my face. I flipped the collar of my Pea Coat up to ward off the wind and ran in long strides across the lot, catching up with my good friend Eddie Adams. Eddie was the visual director for Tradava and, thanks to the task of maintaining the store's display standards over the holiday season, resident grouch.

"Don't tell me her highness is gracing the store with her presence," he said. "Is your sabbatical over already?"

"It was a week of vacation and it's over tomorrow. I came in today to ease my way back into my routine."

"You're afraid the store managers are going to forget they hired you. Out of sight, out of mind."

I'd known Eddie since high school though our friendship had become solid since moving back to the town where I grew up. We shared the same taste in music (80s New Wave) and movies (John Hughes) but were opposites when it came to food territory. (He ate vegetables. I preferred crunchy snack foods, pizza, and anything on Jamie Oliver's "Do Not Eat" list.) I benefitted from his link to the store gossip chain, though I secretly questioned how often he traded gossip about me to maintain the in-and-out flow of insider information.

We flashed our employee IDs and headed to the elevators. "Did you hear anything about Cat?" Eddie asked.

Cat Lestes, the aforementioned friend with a baby, had left town in her third trimester after her husband of ten years had been murdered. We'd been keeping in touch over phone calls emails, and texts, but once the baby arrived, she had considerably less time to chat.

"She had a girl. Six pounds, healthy. Already has orange fuzz on top of her head."

"That is going to be one spoiled baby," he said. I knew he was right.

I changed the subject. "Anything I need to know about the store?"

"Sales, down. Mess, up. Staff, idiots. Stress to booze ratio, two to one."

"I guess that's better than one to two."

He tipped his head and his brows pulled together. He tipped his head the other direction. "Yeah, one to two. That's what I meant."

Eddie held the heavy glass door open for me and then followed me down the corridor. He stopped by his office. "Coffee at eleven?"

"Sounds like a plan."

I rounded the corner and went into the small, two-desk office where *Retrofit for Tradava* operated. My colleague, Nancie Townsend, stood behind her desk with an open cardboard box in front of her.

"Sam! God, I missed you. Come here and give me a hug." She dropped two heavy crystal candlesticks into the box and came out from behind the desk, smothering me in an embrace. "I have news.

4

I can't believe it. I'm engaged! It's like a dream come true. It's perfection!"

"You're engaged?" I asked, instantly regretting the incredulity that snuck into my voice. "Is it—"

"No, not him. You don't know the guy. He's a curator for a small museum in New Mexico. Sweet guy. As sweet as can be. I've never lived in New Mexico—heck, I've never lived west of Ohio! —but sometimes you have to make sacrifices for love."

"You're moving? To New Mexico?" I stepped back from Nancie and took in the desk, the partially empty shelves, and the rather large rock on her left ring finger. "But what about Tradava? And *Retrofit*? You made this magazine what it is. What's going to happen to it?"

Right around my last birthday, I'd been a very overworked employee at a start-up online fashion magazine called *Retrofit*. A series of events led to Tradava acquiring the operation and absorbing us into their advertising wing with the task of putting out a cross between a catalog and a fashion magazine, otherwise known as a magalog.

"We both know I'm not cut out for corporate life in a department store where I have to back trends that were approved in a boardroom. I loved the start-up phase of *Retrofit*. Before we were bought out. We wrote what we wanted to write and worked when we wanted to work. We were allowed to have an opinion. This"— she gestured to the walls around us—"is great for security, but not much else."

"It's too soon for you to leave." I said. "Tradava bought *Retrofit* last year. We haven't had a chance to put our stamp on things."

It hadn't been easy to create cohesive trend stories based on what the buyers had already ordered, but Nancie and I had managed. We had five catalogs completed for the upcoming spring season. It was time to start planning pre-fall. "Now that we're caught up, we're definitely going to have a say in what we feature and how we write about it. That's why they wanted us."

Nancie took my hand and smiled. "Sam, Tradava is your world, not mine." She squeezed my hand and looked down at it. "Is that what I think it is? It's an engagement ring too. To Nick? Nick Taylor? You lucky thing. I knew you two could work it out. Oh my God, we're both engaged. It's double perfection!" She squished me into another hug. "We can both give notice, and because of all the work we did before the holidays, Tradava will have plenty of time to reorganize and do whatever they want to do with the catalog. Everything is going to work out perfectly."

"I don't want to give notice," I said.

Nancie shrugged and went back to packing her box of personal items while I hung up my coat and moved to my desk.

Nancie was a big fan of perfection. She chatted on about how different her life was going to be after she got married, how she planned to help at the museum as unofficial assistant curator, and how she'd need a whole new wardrobe because her current dress code of black and white was a little stark compared to the vibrant colors of the Southwest art scene.

I cued up my email and scribbled a few notes onto my agenda, all the while feeling a growing sense of discontent. Would it work out perfectly? Or was I destined to follow in her footsteps and become Mrs. Nick Taylor, the wife of a popular shoe designer, who lacked her own identity?

2

EMERGING FASHION TRENDS

*N*ick's career was on the verge of breaking out. His shoes were featured regularly on the editorial pages of major fashion magazines. I'd first met him eleven years ago when I worked as a designer shoe buyer in New York. That path had led me to career success but not happiness, so after nine years, I'd left.

In that nine years, Nick's reputation had grown. I didn't doubt he wanted the best for me, but on more than one occasion my path veered widely from his, often into slightly dangerous territory. I never looked for trouble, but something inside me didn't walk away when I found it.

That's what bothered me the most: that I still hadn't found what I was looking for. My job had become something for me to grab ahold of and I found that I needed it. Would professional Samantha be able to coexist with married Samantha? Would Nick's growing fame eclipse my accomplishments?

I provided the minimal responses needed to keep Nancie talking even though my mind was miles away. Somewhere between her pro/con list on bolo ties (retro enough to be cool or too Stray Cats?) she was interrupted by a call. She answered, said "of course" three times, and hung up.

"That was Human Resources. Looks like they got my letter of resignation. Wish me luck!"

"Good luck," I said, with what little enthusiasm I could muster. I returned to my overflowing inbox, unread emails, and growing sense of threatened identity.

An email from Nick popped up and I opened it. It was a forwarded message from Nick's showroom manager, Angela, and included pictures of empty, run down factories. The one line from Nick said, *see what you're missing?*

While I considered the appropriate response—a balance between *looks like fun* and *I have my own life!* —I clicked onto the next email. And suddenly, things looked a little brighter.

To: Samantha Kidd
Fr: Carl Collins
Re: Interview/Profile
Sam: I pitched a series of feel-good local celebrity profiles to the Sunday Times and got the green light this morning. After your involvement in the recent crime wave over the holidays, we all agreed you'd be the ideal candidate to kick off the series. If you're interested, I'll send over the release forms and we can set up the interview and photo shoot.

Carl Collins was a reporter for the local paper. He was in his mid-thirties but dressed to appear older to inspire trust in a span of generations. He was determined to become the Tom Wolfe of Ribbon, Pennsylvania, and somehow knowing me fit into that master plan.

On any other occasion, I'd see right through Carl's motivation. He wanted to butter me up so I'd tip him off the next time I was involved in something newsworthy. But this time I had my motivation: protect my identity from being overshadowed by Nick's. There was a very good chance this wasn't how "healthy relationship" stuff was supposed to work, but not having had many successful, long-term relationships under my patent-leather belt, I went with my gut. Which actually *was* under my patent-leather belt.

I replied yes, thanks, please email releases, and then clicked send. Almost immediately the documents showed up in my inbox with a note: *I'll be in touch. -CC*

I starred the email and moved on to my next task: looking for emerging fashion trends. I checked social media, clicked through stills of recent fashion shows, and paged through backup copies of *Women's Wear Daily.* It was my unrefined method for filtering a whole lot of stimulus into a clear message for the store. And like I'd told Nancie, it was early enough on the calendar that we would have a chance to suggest editorial stories in the next catalog, not react to those dictated to us.

I opened a blank sketchpad and filled the first page with notes: *ladylike suiting. Colorful. Tailored. Chic. Return to Camelot. Early Sixties.* Fully dressed and accessorized. As I scribbled the free-form stream of consciousness triggered by the websites and fashion coverage I'd reviewed, a possible ad campaign came into focus. A barren, concrete, bombed-out factory background with models in candy-colored suits. It would be the perfect way to show off the trend that was popping up in several designer collections. Easy to accessorize: black tights and shoes to set off the colorful suits. Leather gloves. Hats. Sunglasses to play into the Jackie Kennedy vibe. The store would love the concept because it included merchandise from multiple departments, all the better to drive sales.

Tradava had sponsored a couple of fashion-industry-related events since I'd been back in Ribbon, establishing themselves as more than a store with fishing gear and freshly baked goods. New designers invited our buyers to view their collections, and once in a blue moon, the store negotiated an exclusive.

In terms of business growth, it was a natural for the store to shift advertising focus onto the trend market. The more we competed with online retailers like Amazon, the more we had to come up with a hook to get people to walk through our doors.

Every advertising spread had to be approved by senior management, and approval was based on details like cost of location, transportation, models, et cetera. Apparel shoots had the highest budget because they required models and exotic backdrops. That also made them the most difficult to pitch. But I had an idea that almost guaranteed senior management would say yes.

I'd invite Carl Collins to do the interview at a mock photo shoot and stick around for a behind-the-scenes peek at how we put the catalog together. Tradava would get extra exposure, Carl would get something entirely unique for the *Ribbon Times*, and I'd secure my place as a local celebrity and not as Mrs. Nick Taylor.

I printed the forms and hastily filled them out, and then called the General Merchandise Manager of Ladies Apparel to set up a brief meeting.

"Pam Trotter's office," said a female voice. It had a slightly high pitched nasally tone, and I recognized the executive's assistant.

"Is this Wanda? It's Samantha Kidd, from the advertising department." We spent about a minute on small talk—how was your vacation, great, yours? —before I cut to the chase. "I'm working on the pre-fall catalog and had an idea I wanted to pitch. Does Pam have any time on her calendar this week? I don't need more than fifteen minutes."

"Can you come right now?"

What? Now? I needed concept boards and background sets and locations to pitch and ballpark cost estimates. I was not ready.

"Sure," I said.

"Great. Better get here fast because she's got projections starting at ten."

"On my way." I grabbed my notebook, cell phone, and the open copy of *WWD* and ran to the elevator.

Pam Trotter was in her late fifties and wore it well. Her auburn hair was layered just enough to give it movement around her face, but not so much that it distracted from her clear blue eyes. She wore a navy blue turtleneck sweater and wide legged trousers, and her sunglasses were perched on top of her head, I assumed more as an accessory than because the store was bright. An unstructured navy blue tweed blazer was draped on the back of her office chair. She flipped back and forth between the first few pages of my sketchpad with her left hand while her right gently rubbed at the heavy links on her gold chain necklace.

"You came up with this just now?" she asked.

"This morning. I was reviewing the runway shows and the looks that were trending on social media and it just clicked." I bit my lower lip. "I'd have to do some research to scout a factory, but I have a lead. My boyfr—fia—Nick Taylor sent me pictures of a couple of available spaces. If you like the idea, I can make some calls and work up a budget. If we act fast, we could get this shoot in the can in the next week. That'll allow the buyers more time to prepare their pitches for the rest of the catalog."

"I love it," Pam said. "It's fresh and exactly what's happening right now. All this grunge, yuck." She wrinkled her nose. "I love the first catalog of the season. Everything looks so new. I just wish we didn't have to wait until July to see it in print."

"I had an idea about that too," I said. In as few words as possible, I told her about the interview for the paper and my thoughts about the proposed photo shoot. "It would give Tradava extra press for free. It would be a teaser for customers who could come in and place advance orders for the merchandise, and it would be a way for us to claim ownership of this trend before it hit the rest of the pre-fall market. We wouldn't have to hire models, just move merchandise from here to the site and someone from the store's shipping and delivery department could do that. We'd get a jump on the rest of the fashion publications."

Pam removed her sunglasses from her head, folded the wands in, and tucked them into the top right drawer of her desk. "It's brilliant," she said, though her tone was matter-of-fact. "Assuming we can get samples from the designers. Tights, gloves, sunglasses can all be pulled from inventory. Designers can overnight us their runway samples of the suits. The problem is the shoes."

She was right. Retail buyers selected their advertising choices at market in December. The factories produced those samples early so stores would have time to shoot them but anything we requested now wouldn't get produced until after the orders were fulfilled and that would be far too late.

"We could pull from stock," she added, "but that would take

away from the high fashion angle. "What's happening in footwear is almost as important as what's happening in ready-to-wear."

Seeing as how I'd been playing with forty pair of shoes from Nick's upcoming shoe collection for the past week, I already knew what the key shoe trends were going to be. Platforms. Square toes. Stilettos. For as feminine as the clothes were, the shoes had an edge. Like so many other aspects of fashion, it was the contradiction in styles that made them work. I could ask Nick to produce the shoes for us in exchange for editorial credit. And I knew he'd say yes. But I didn't know if he'd say yes because it was good for him or because it was good for me.

This relationship stuff was hard.

Pam signed off on my releases and checked her watch. "I've got pre-projections starting in about five minutes. Lock down the factory first and then get me a concept board. We'll figure the shoe thing out. Good work, Samantha." She smiled, and I left.

By the time I returned to the advertising offices, I was brimming with excitement. This was big. This was bigger than big. This was huge. It was the perfect high profile project to make everybody at Tradava take notice of me and possibly even erase some of the damage from what had happened the first time I tried to work here. I'd have to warn Carl to avoid mention of that in his interview.

The office was empty when I returned. Nancie's cardboard box was gone and the shelves behind her desk had been picked clean of personal belongings. The thing that remained was a paper cube printed with her original *Retrofit* logo. The top square of paper had her phone number, followed by *xoxoxo*. I pulled the piece of paper off and tucked it into my wallet. I didn't want to lose touch with her, but I knew how retail friendships were. Tight while you're there in front of each other, but out of sight, out of mind.

I moved to my desk. A note had been scribbled on the middle of my desk blotter that said, "Party's over! Booze ratio just went up. Call me."

It was a few minutes past eleven, so if I'd missed Eddie it hadn't been by much. I called his extension and left a message.

I scanned in the documents and emailed them to Carl with a

note outlining my idea and a barely concealed threat if he didn't use it. I pulled up Nick's email with the factory pictures and scrolled through, looking for contact or location information. When I found none, I called him. He didn't answer. I texted twice, sent an email, and finally called Angela, his showroom manager.

"Angela, it's Samantha. I was hoping to get some info on the factories Nick is visiting today."

"Thank God you called," she said. "He wants you to join him, but I don't have your new number."

"Are you sure? The last time we talked, he didn't want me there."

"Since when do you listen to what he says?" Angela said. "But I'm sure. He said it was urgent and that was two hours ago. I think something might be wrong. If I were you, I'd drop everything and go."

3

AN ENGAGEMENT GIFT

A surge of adrenaline shot through my arms and legs. I jumped up from my desk while still holding the phone to my ear. "Which factory?" I asked. "Where?"

"It's in the old Prince district, by Cherry and South Sixth," Angela said.

"I'm on my way." I hung up and grabbed my coat and bag and left, almost colliding with Eddie. He held a thermal take-out cup in each hand, and our near-accident resulted in splattered coffee on his New Order T-shirt.

"Dude!" he said. "You are not going to believe what happened. Seriously. Do these people think I'm a robot?"

"Can't talk. Emergency. Gotta go."

Eddie held out one of the cups. "Take this. I'll catch up with you later."

I grabbed the coffee and raced out of the store.

Nick didn't answer either of the calls I made on my way to the factory district. It was a ten-minute drive and after two attempts to reach him, I tossed my phone onto the passenger seat and concentrated on driving fast. I took the Penn Avenue exit and blitzed through the downtown streets until I found the factory where

Angela said he'd gone. Leaving a message with Angela and not calling directly was out of character. Something was up.

Nick's white pickup truck was parked in the lot in the space closest to the entrance. A shiny black Lexus was parked next to him. I parked next to the Lexus and ran inside.

"Nick?" I yelled. "Nick, can you hear me?" I ran into the center of the factory and spun in a circle, looking for signs of a factory-related-urgent-but-not-911-worthy situation that would have changed Nick's mind about wanting me there.

"Kidd?" Nick said. I looked around, trying to place the location of his voice. "What are you doing here?"

I looked up. He was on a narrow platform about ten feet above me. Next to him was a short man in a black coat and hat. Nick was easily six inches taller than the man, but considering their location, I was having a hard time judging either of their heights.

"Are you okay?" I asked.

"Yes, I'm okay. Wait right there. I'm coming down." He turned to the man next to him and said something and then disappeared.

I met him by the base of the stairs and threw my arms around him. He gently pushed me away. "What are you doing here?"

"I need a factory for work. I called Angela and she said you were trying to reach me, that it was urgent, and I had to get here right away. I thought—" I stopped talking. The echo of my voice bounced off the exposed concrete, sounding hollow and panicky. Nick wouldn't call me if there was something wrong. He'd call the police. "I don't know what I thought. Why am I here?"

"You're not kidding around, are you?" he said. This time Nick put his arms around me. "You want to slow down and fill me in?"

"Like I said, I need a factory. The one in the picture you sent this morning looked like it would work, so I called Angela to get the address. Before I had a chance to tell her why I called, she said you told her you wanted me to meet you here. I've been calling you to find out why you changed your mind, but you didn't answer."

"The building is made of concrete. Blocks the signal."

"Oh."

"Besides, I didn't tell Angela I wanted you here. I told her *you* wanted to be here."

"Oh," I said again.

The man who'd been standing next to Nick on the landing upstairs had joined us on the ground floor. He cleared his throat. I'd temporarily forgotten that, for Nick, this was a business meeting. I stepped backward, out of Nick's arms and held out my hand. "I'm sorry to have interrupted your meeting in such an unprofessional manner. I'm Samantha Kidd."

"Vito," the man said. He grasped my hand with his gloved one and shook it. "You work for Mr. Taylor?"

"Samantha is my fiancé," Nick said.

Vito smiled. "I did not know you had become engaged. Congratulations! We'll toast at our next meeting."

"There's not going to be a next meeting, Vito. I told you, I'm not ready to move my production from Italy to Ribbon." He put his hands up. "I hear what you're saying about bringing jobs back to the US, but for now, I'm going to keep things the way they are."

Vito shrugged his shoulders as if Nick's response didn't faze him one way or the other. He turned to me. "I believe the lady said she's in need of a factory?"

Well, this was awkward. I looked at Nick, who raised his eyebrows. My earlier fears about loss of identity seemed trite considering I'd charged into the place like Wonder Woman prepared to save her man from an unknown threat.

"I'm setting up a photo shoot for a local department store. For their catalog. I pitched the idea of using an empty factory as the backdrop. The general merchandise manager signed off on the concept and told me to make the arrangements. So here I am."

Nick crossed his arms over his coat. "I think I can help you find another location that would work."

Vito spoke. "Don't be hasty, Nick. This is your fiancé. The woman you're going to marry. You want her to be happy, yes?" He held out an arm and guided me toward the back of the factory. "I think we can work something out. When would your team need access?"

"Um," I looked over my shoulder at Nick, who shook his head back and forth. I looked back at Vito. "I don't think I should make a decision right this second."

"I tell you what. You put in a good word with your future husband, tell him to reconsider his decision, and I'll let you use my factory for as many photo shoots as you want. No charge."

"That's not necessary. Nick and I have separate businesses and separate lives. My interests in your factory are strictly on behalf of Tradava. We're prepared to pay to rent the space, just like we would for any photo shoot."

"No, no, no. Consider it an engagement gift." He raised my bare hand to his lips and kissed it. "Until next time, Ms. Kidd. It's been a pleasure."

The pleasure was all his. I pulled my hand away and surreptitiously wiped it on the back of my coat. Vito approached Nick, shook his hand, and left.

The factory was awkwardly silent except for the sound of Vito's heels snapping against the cement. As if by unspoken agreement, neither Nick or I spoke until Vito's car engine started and the black Lexus swung out of the parking lot.

"What did he say to you?" Nick asked.

"He wants me to ask you to reconsider your decision. But don't worry, I told him our lives and our businesses were separate and that I was here acting on behalf of Tradava."

"Kidd, I don't think this is a good idea."

"Whoa," I said, and put my hands up. "My idea is *very* good. The GMM of Tradava practically gave me a promotion when she heard it. I'll look at other factories, but if this is the best one, I'll have Vito draw up a contract and we'll rent it, just like we do with everybody else. You don't have any say in that."

"That's not what I meant. You always have good ideas. That's what makes you special, because you see things differently than the rest of the world. It's just—there's a history with this factory and with Vito, and it's not particularly pleasant."

"A history? Like a Saturday night special?" I *knew* empty factories were exciting. I leaned forward and looked back into the dark interior.

Nick shook his head. "No more *Godfather* movies for you."

I straightened up. "I'll call Vito tomorrow and let him know the store lined up something else. Okay?"

"Thanks."

Until that moment, I expected Nick to say I should do whatever it was I wanted to do. The fact that I'd given in to his request triggered the same fears from earlier. I looked out at the parking lot for a moment, and then back at Nick. "You should call Angela and straighten this out."

He held up his finger and tapped his phone. The call rang seven times before he disconnected and tried again. Same thing—Angela didn't answer. I walked a few steps toward the exit.

"Kidd, hold up." He put his phone in his pocket and jogged to me.

"I'll get out of here and let you get on with your day. I was so excited after I had the factory idea that my mind has been going a mile a minute."

"It does that," he said. "This factory thing—it *is* a good idea. Angela has a whole file of local factory sites. I'll bring it to dinner tonight and maybe you can get a lead from there."

"You told Vito you weren't planning on moving your production out of Italy, so why the folder on factories?"

Nick hesitated for a moment and seemed to consider his words. "I'm not convinced Vito would make the best business partner, but he's right about one thing. There are tax incentives available to me if I create jobs in the US. Ribbon is the perfect setting. Lots of these factories have been sitting around collecting dust. I could have my labels produced here and shipped to Italy or have the tissue paper from the boxes produced here, or even the boxes themselves. Think about it. There's a reason Paper Mill Road is named paper mill road. Just because the paper mills are currently closed, doesn't mean they can't be reopened too."

I drove back toward Tradava, but it was after lunch and all I'd had all day was coffee. I exited the highway, but instead of taking the shortcut to the store, went through the light, into the parking lot for the strip mall where my favorite sandwich shop sat. And since it just happened to be a few doors down from Nick's showroom, I could check on Angela, pick up the factory file and work on securing a location this afternoon. Three birds, one stone. Samantha 2.0 productivity at its best.

I parked close to the showroom and yanked on the door. It was locked. I rattled it a couple of times and pressed my face up to the glass, looking for Angela. It was the middle of the day. She was probably in the ladies' room. I flipped through my key ring for the one Nick had made for me back when I worked for him and prayed he hadn't changed the locks. The key slipped in and the door pulled open.

"Angela?" I called out. "It's Samantha. I used my key." Her desk was neat, and her computer screen was dark. A manila folder labeled FACTORIES sat on top of her desk. I flipped the folder open and fanned out a list of addresses that was several pages long.

I walked through the showroom to the small kitchenette, and then poked my head into the tiny office ick used when he wanted privacy. No Angela. She'd probably slipped out for a bite and would return in a few minutes. I went back to her desk and copied the files from the folder on the small machine behind her desk, put the originals back in the folder, and stuffed the duplicates into my handbag.

I slipped off my black bootie. While I waited for Angela to return, I wandered around the showroom on lopsided heel heights, occasionally slipping on one of Nick's shoe samples and checking out my reflection in the knee-high mirrors he'd strategically placed. It was while trying on a black suede platform pump that I noticed the blood reflected in the mirror.

I turned around and scanned the showroom floor, looking for the source. It came from the sample closet to the left of Angela's desk. A nauseating sensation started in my stomach and radiated outward, causing my arms to twitch and my hands to shake. I hobbled to the closet and eased the door open.

Angela's body fell out.

4

MAFIA PRINCESS

I threw my arms out to catch her. Her dead weight knocked me backward two steps. My hands were sticky from her blood, blood that transferred onto my clothes. I let go and her stiff and cold body fell onto the floor, the sound muffled by the carpet where she landed.

The phone on the desk started to ring. I stared at it for a moment, temporarily at a loss for which direction to turn. I had to call the police, but this was Nick's place of business. I let his service answer and pulled my phone out of my handbag. The sight of the blood on my fingers made me woozy. I hit Emergency at the bottom of my lock screen. When the call connected, I reported the body and the location.

There was nothing for me to do but wait. I wanted to clean myself but knew it was better for the police to see things as I'd found them. If evidence had transferred from Angela's body to mine when she fell from the closet, I didn't want to be responsible for it going down the drain of Nick's sink.

The phone on Angela's desk rang on, fraying my nerves. The number was blocked, and the service wasn't picking up. Angela couldn't do her job, but I could. I picked up the receiver.

"Nick Taylor Designs," I said. There was a pause on the other end. "Hello? You've reached Nick Taylor's showroom. Can I help you?"

"Kidd?"

"Nick?" Oh, no. No, no, no, no, no. I did not want to be the person to deliver this news. Not to him. Not now. Not ever.

"What are you doing answering Angela's phone?"

"Nick—"

"I thought you were going back to work. Why are you at my showroom?"

"Nick—"

"Is Angela there? Put her on the phone."

"Nick, I can't. She's dead. Somebody killed her and hid her body in the sample closet. I'm so sorry." I didn't realize I'd repeated the last phrase three times or that I'd started to cry.

"Kidd, get out of there."

"I can't do that either. The police are on their way."

"So am I."

We both hung up. The phone rang almost instantly. I picked up the receiver, expecting Nick again. The line was quiet. Just in case, I inhaled sharply to get my breathing under control. "Nick Taylor Designs," I said.

"Angie?" asked a male voice.

"No. Who is this?" I asked.

"Put Angie on the phone."

"Who are you and what do you want?"

The phone was silent for a few seconds and then the voice returned. "Your boyfriend is not a nice man. You tell him he better watch his step. Do you understand what I'm saying?"

"You won't get away with this," I said. "The police will find you. They'll arrest you for murder. I'll make sure of that."

"Make sure you give your boyfriend the message." *Click.*

I dropped into Angela's chair. I was still holding the receiver in my hand when the police arrived.

After being attended to by the medical techs and then trading my soiled shirt, blazer, and leather leggings for generic blue scrubs, I was told I could wash and wait in Nick's office. There was so much wrong with the past hour I didn't know where to start.

I called Tradava and left a message with the operator that I wouldn't be returning to the store, and that if I was needed, I could be reached by cell. Autonomy was one small perk of working mostly independently in our small catalog department. The news would be public soon enough, and the likelihood of keeping my name out of it was slim. Nick had yet to arrive, or if he had, he was being kept out front, away from the crime scene.

I heard someone approach. "Ms. Kidd," said a familiar voice.

"Detective Loncar." I spun the swivel chair around and looked up at Ribbon, Pennsylvania's senior homicide detective.

Detective Loncar and I had first met after I'd discovered the body of my boss in an elevator at Tradava. Since then, we'd slipped into a comfortable co-existence. I'd learned about his marital problems, he'd learned about my fears of commitment. In the most unexpected, unencouraged, and often unwanted manner possible, he was sort of a father figure to me. My father was out in California somewhere with my mom, enjoying retirement and the unencumberment of dependent children and mortgage payments (and people who use words that don't exist.)

I wasn't sure what to expect from Detective Loncar today. The last time I'd been involved in something like this, he'd been in Tahiti. It was a move so out of character that I feared he'd gotten a Queer Eye makeover while I wasn't looking. I glanced down at his shoes.

Nope, same Detective Loncar.

He turned around and grabbed the back of a chair on casters and rolled it toward me. He sat down. He leaned forward and put his elbows on his thighs and folded his hands together. I waited. He finally looked from the floor up to my face.

"I don't like this one," he said.

"I don't like any of them."

He sat up. "Angela di Sotto was the daughter of a woman rumored to be a mob mistress. Nobody has ever linked Angela to the business, but she has recently been seen in the company of

Jimmy the Tomato, and that raises questions. I know one of my men took your statement. What I need to know is if you can tell me anything that'll give me a direction? I've seen a lot of crime in this city, and the department has been doing what we can to dissuade the mob from moving in, but I gotta say, I never expected a mafia princess to show up dead in a shoe store."

"Showroom," I corrected. It was my first contribution to the conversation, except for the not-liking-murder thing, which was sort of a no-brainer. "I already told your officer this, but right after I found the body, the phone started ringing. I called 911 and made the report, but after I hung up, I kept thinking this is Nick's business and if someone was trying to reach him, it was poor form for me to let the phone go unanswered."

"Mr. Taylor told me he spoke to you."

"He's here? Where?" I stood up and looked over Detective Loncar's head.

"He's in the parking lot. I can't let him inside. He'll potentially corrupt the crime scene. We have to go over everything before we let him, or anybody else, in."

"Or let me out. I can't leave, can I?"

He looked at my blue scrubs. "That's not what you were wearing when you found Ms. di Sotto, is it?"

"Scrubs? When have you ever seen me wear scrubs?"

"Where are your clothes?"

"One of your officers took them. He put them in a plastic bag and said I'd get them back after they were analyzed for forensic evidence. I'm not going to say something insensitive about how my pants were leather and should be kept free of chemicals that might damage them. I'm not going to tell you that my jacket was wool and my shirt was Egyptian cotton and both might be ruined if you don't treat them right. I don't care if I ever see that outfit again. But I do want my other bootie."

"Why'd my officer take one of your shoes?"

"I was trying on samples when I saw the puddle of blood coming out from the closet. I didn't stop to put my bootie back on."

"I'll have one of my officers look for it."

23

I sat back down and studied Detective Loncar. His Tahiti tan had faded and creases that came after too much sun lined his face. Dark circles showed under his eyes. His thinning hair was cut short and slightly longer on one side than the other, like he'd done it himself with a pair of trimmers. All this time I'd held out hopes that his trip to Tahiti had been a reconciliation with his wife. It saddened me to think he was still on the outs with her.

"Detective, there was a second call after Nick and I hung up. It was a man. He asked me to put Angela on the phone and when I asked who he was, he said to give Nick a message. He said to warn him to watch his step."

"What step?"

"I don't know."

Loncar looked angry. "This isn't the time to play games, Ms. Kidd. If you know something, you tell me. Now."

"You think I think this is a game? You just told me Nick's office manager was involved with the juice man for the local mafia. Now she's dead. What part of that sounds like a game?"

He glared at me.

"You said tomato. My mind went to juice."

He stood up and pulled a card out of his wallet.

"I already have your card," I said.

"Take it anyway."

I followed Loncar out of Nick's office to the main portion of the showroom. The bright lime green walls were too cheery for what had taken place here. People shouldn't be capable of murder in a lime green room filled with modern furniture and designer shoes.

Loncar approached the officer who had taken my clothes and said something to him. The officer pointed to my bootie, sitting alone on top of Angela's desk. Loncar put his hand in a plastic bag and picked it up, turned it over, and examined the sole. He looked at me and shook his head, and then turned the plastic bag inside out with my bootie inside.

Nick stood on the sidewalk outside the showroom. He saw me and came closer. I put my open palm on the inside of the window. He pulled his glove off his hand and placed it opposite mine. I had an uncomfortable sense that this was what it would be like if I ever had to visit Nick in jail, but quickly dismissed the thought. Nick was too good to do anything to end up in jail. If one of us was to be the future incarcerated in this relationship, we all knew it was me.

I suspected we'd be able to hear each other through the glass, but as if by mutual agreement, neither of us spoke. We stood there, two hands separated by a storefront window.

Loncar came over and told me I could leave. Yellow plastic crime scene tape had been attached to the door to the sample closet and wrapped around Angela's desk. The closet itself had been sealed.

I hobbled out of the shop behind two uniformed officers with Loncar behind me. The scent of cured sandwich meat hung in the air. The number of cars in the lot had doubled thanks to curious customers who had come to the strip mall for hoagies and stayed for a story to tell tonight at dinner.

"Ms. Kidd, how did you enter the showroom?" Loncar asked.

"I have a key," I said.

"I thought you gave that back?" Nick asked.

"I made copies."

Nick frowned. Loncar pointed to the door. "One of you two needs to lock up so we can seal the door."

"But how is Nick supposed to get back in?" I asked.

"Mr. Taylor," Loncar said to Nick even though I'd asked the question, "I hope to be able to release your showroom to you tomorrow, but until you hear from me, nobody is to go in. Not you, not your...," now he looked at me, "not Ms. Kidd. I don't care if Imelda Marcos shows up. If you haven't heard from me personally, then you don't go through that door."

"I'll do anything I can to cooperate." Nick looked at me. "So will Ms. Kidd. Right, Ms. Kidd?"

"Detective Loncar already knows everything I know."

Loncar stepped away and pulled out his phone. Nick took off his overcoat and draped it around me. "What were you doing here?"

"I came by to get the file on the factories. You said Angela had it and since I agreed not to use Vito's, I thought I could find a replacement this afternoon."

Loncar stopped and turned around. "Did you say Vito?"

"Yes. Why?" I said.

He walked back. "Vito Cantone?"

This time Nick spoke. "Yes. Why?"

"What business did you have with Vito Cantone?" Loncar asked Nick.

"He wanted me to consider moving my production to one of his vacant factories. Why?"

Loncar looked at me. "Did you know this?"

I threw my hands in the air. "I didn't even know the man's last name! Why is that important?"

"Because Vito Cantone was Angela di Sotto's last boyfriend."

5

CABBAGE

"That little man from this morning used to date Angela? He's so old!" I said.

Loncar's expression tightened up. His mouth pulled into a little knot and his forehead creased. "Vito Cantone is a year younger than me."

"No way," I said quickly. "I thought you were my age."

Nick tucked his chin and stifled a smile.

"Mr. Taylor," Loncar said, ignoring me, "I'm going to need to speak to you about Ms. di Sotto. How's tomorrow morning?"

Nick looked at the officers sealing the door to his store. "Pretty sure my schedule is wide open."

They coordinated a time and place and Loncar left. I wrapped my arms around Nick's torso and laid my head on his chest. "I didn't expect them to make you stand out here. I should have. Shouldn't I have known that? If they'd let you into your showroom or if they'd keep you out? After all this time, I should know that, right?"

"Shhhhh," Nick said. "Let's get out of the cold."

I shrugged out of Nick's coat and climbed into the truck, and then pulled the coat over me like a blanket. I hadn't looked at a clock while waiting inside Nick's showroom, so I was surprised to discover from the clock on Nick's dashboard that it was after six. I hadn't had a meal since breakfast and my nerves felt it.

"Sit here and get warm. Your convertible will take a lot longer to heat up than my truck." He pulled me across the front seat and shifted his coat so it covered both of us.

"Angela was always nice to me. When did you hire her?"

"Last year, after my dad broke his hip. It was around the same time he moved in with me. She was a godsend—taking care of things when I couldn't."

"Do you think she was trying to tell me something when she sent me out to meet you?"

"No, I still think that was a mix-up. I asked her to send those pictures to you and then you called her. I could see that it looked to her like I wanted you to join me."

"But while you and I were at the factory, someone came here and killed her. And then hid her body in the sample closet where you would have found her." I shivered, and Nick put his arms around me. "Do you think her murder had something to do with your shoe company? Is someone going to come after you next?"

"I don't know what to think right now."

I leaned against him. "Who would shoot someone in broad daylight and then put them in a closet? Who would be so bold as to think they would get away with that?" I asked.

"A bad one."

We were both quiet for a moment. The interior of the windows grew foggy from our breathing. I reached forward and pressed my thumb into the condensation, leaving a small oblong fingerprint through which to see.

"Do you know how to reach her family?"

Nick was silent for a few seconds. "Yes," he finally said. "Her mom died when she was young, just like mine did, but one time she mentioned she had family in West Ribbon. I don't think they were close." We sat in the relative warmth of the truck, both of us staring at the fogged-up window.

"What happens next?" I asked.

"I don't know the full implications, but for now, I'll have to move any appointments on the showroom schedule. I could rent a suite at a local hotel and use it as a temporary showroom, but with the samples locked up here, I don't know if there's much of a reason to reschedule. I'll have to hire a new showroom manager, but that can wait. Right now, let's talk about you. Tell me about your first day back at Tradava."

I wasn't surprised by Nick's not-so-subtle attempt to steer the conversation another direction. I'd long ago learned that his concern sometimes trickled into overprotective zone, and the murder of his assistant at his showroom had to have left him feeling guilty. Nick never liked when I got involved in police matters, and this time the police matter involved him. But there was something else tonight. Something he wasn't saying. He was holding back, and I didn't know why.

"You don't want to talk about Angela?"

"Kidd, I can't begin to imagine what it was like for Angela in the last minutes of her life, or what it was like for you to open that closet and have her body fall out. I'm doing my best to change the subject."

"To be honest, I don't feel much like talking about Tradava right now. Do you mind if we just sit here quietly?"

He bent down and kissed my cheek. "Of course I don't mind."

Half an hour later, warmed to the core, I climbed out of Nick's truck and into my coupe. It was in remarkably good shape for a car from the late nineties, thanks to the difficulties of driving around New York City during the nine years I'd lived there and the convenience of writing a monthly check to pay for covered parking. I postponed our tentative plans for dinner and drove home. I wanted to shower and curl up in bed with my cat. Nick understood.

The next morning, I woke to my ringing cell phone. I unplugged it from the charger and answered, my voice still thick with sleep.

"Hullo?" I said.

"Kidd? I can't believe you held out on me. I thought we had an agreement. Did yesterday mean nothing to you?"

I sat up. Logan lifted his head and meowed in annoyance. "Who is this?"

"It's Carl Collins from the *Ribbon Times*. You found the body of Angela di Sotto and you didn't call me? I'm hurt, Kidd. I'm half tempted to pull the plug on our interview."

"Carl. Hold on." I set the phone down on my pink sheets and rubbed my hands over my face. After three deep inhale/exhale breaths, I picked the phone back up. "Okay, I'm back."

"Are you still in bed? It's six forty-five. How long do you normally sleep?"

"I get up at seven forty-five like a normal person." Eight. Eight-ish. Eight thirty if I showered the night before. "Who calls at six forty-five?"

"Answer a couple of questions for me and I'll let you get back to your beauty sleep. I know Angela was found dead in Nick Taylor's showroom, but the cops are playing this one close to the hip. When did she die? How did she die? You knew her. Was there any evidence of illness prior to her death? Or was it a suicide? Pills. Overdose. Was that it? Did she tell you anything before she died?"

"How much coffee have you already had?"

"I don't drink coffee. Slows me down."

"Yeah, I can see how that might be a problem."

"Keep it up, Kidd. Just remember, the sooner you give me a statement, the sooner you can go back to sleep."

"Carl, have you ever stopped to think there might be a reason the police are playing this close to the hip?"

"Sure. Angela has mob connections."

"How do you know that?"

"She's been seen with Vito Cantone at least half a dozen times and members of her family were named in that high profile case that took Lucky Vincenzo to trial."

Lucky Vincenzo was a well-known New York businessman who'd made no secret of his underworld connections. He'd been tied to gambling, racketeering, prostitution, and bootlegging. He'd also owned a sizeable portion of the garment district, which brought him the reputation of local kid done good. He'd been arrested and bailed out half a dozen times, the streak ending after he'd been fatally wounded during a mass shooting outside the courthouse last year. Nobody knew who, if anyone, had taken charge of Lucky's territories in the wake of his death. The police had not been able to link the shooter to the mafia, and the killing had been ruled accidental. The unanswered questions added to his legend.

"You're planning on exposing this in your article?"

"Nope. That's cabbage."

"You lost me."

"Cabbage. Old news. It's been written, tossed, and chewed on by the local rodents. I need something I can print today. Unless you're saying this was a mob hit…?"

He was looking for confirmation that he could print. "I'm not saying anything. Not until after I've had something to eat."

I hung up and threw the covers back.

I'd read a recent article about habits of highly productive people and had been trying to incorporate them into my life. One of the habits was getting up earlier. This morning, Carl's unexpected call had done the trick.

The memory of finding Angela yesterday came at me unexpectedly. I pictured her body falling forward and the blood that had transferred onto my hands. Somebody had come into Nick's studio, shot her, and stuffed her in the sample closet. Had she known her killer? Considering what people were saying about her, it seemed likely. And if what Carl said was right, I doubted Angela could have dated a mob man without knowing his business. She'd never seemed that dumb.

I showered, dressed in black tights, black pumps, and a fit-and-flare navy blue sweater dress that landed just above my knees. If Carl knew about Angela's death, then it was in the news. Regardless of what I'd learned of her life over the past twelve hours, my relationship with her was as Nick's office manager. We'd shared coffee breaks and dished about *Project Runway*, shopped at the same outlets and sometimes even shared Friends and Family discounts. Angela and I hadn't exactly been best buddies, but we were close enough that it would be a nice gesture to pay my respects to her family after work.

I fed Logan, cleaned his litter box, and spent ten minutes encouraging him to chase a red laser pointer around the living room for exercise. I suspected I'd find him asleep on my cashmere sweaters when I got home. He'd learned how to open the closet while I was gone, and I was tempted to set up a hidden camera to catch him in action.

Eddie was waiting for me in my office. "It's about time. Is everything okay? Dude. Spill." He slid a cup of coffee toward me.

"That was not how my first day back at work was supposed to go. I came in to get a jump start. I made all the right resolutions too. It's a new year and a new me. And it started so well. I even impressed Pam Trotter in an impromptu meeting yesterday morning."

"I heard. Photo shoot in one of the abandoned factories by Canal Street, right?"

"How'd you hear?"

"Good ideas get repeated. I heard you pitched the photo shoot and linked it to an article in the *Ribbon Times*. For what it's worth, everybody loved it. Somebody even said you're one to watch. Perfect timing, too."

I warmed at the praise. "I'm just glad they finally got past their first impression of me. What do you mean about timing?"

"The owners are coming to the store."

"The Tradavas are doing a store visit? When?"

"Wednesday."

"But the store is in the middle of post-holiday sales."

"I know." Eddie slumped in his chair.

Store visits were a dreaded part of the retail culture. Executives high enough on the totem pole to have forgotten what happens during business as usual set up a schedule of store visits. They meet with senior management, walk the selling floors, chat up the associates, and mingle with customers. The idea is to put a face to the name of the store. It's also to make sure the store is performing at peak level. It's amazing what executives will notice when they look at us from their view at the top.

Possibly the worst byproduct of a visit was the pressure on the employees to make the store appear perfect. Sales associates were instructed to dress their professional best, hide their coffee cups, answer every ringing phone within two rings, and make sure there wasn't a speck of dust in sight. The real grunt work fell on the shoulders of the visual department and managers. I suspected Eddie was about to start talking like Scarface again.

"This is my last moment of peace before I crack the whip out there. What's going on with you?"

"Long story or short story?"

"How long until your coworker shows up?"

"Nancie gave notice yesterday. We've got the office to ourselves."

"Long version, please." He took the lid off his coffee and swallowed several gulps.

I gave him the highlights from twenty-two and a half hours ago: my research into the recent runway shows, Carl's interview request for the *Ribbon Times*, and Nick's email with pictures of factories. "Everything clicked."

"Trask-radio," he said.

"Exactly. I went to see Pam, pitched her the idea, and she said to go for it."

"Are you sure this whole idea wasn't because you knew Nick was looking at factories and you could spend more time with him? You're not going to become one of those boring married people who only do things together, are you?"

I put down my coffee and gave him my best watch-it-buster stare. "I've been involved in six criminal investigations in two years. The overwhelming stack of evidence seems to indicate that 'boring' might not be all that bad."

"Good point."

"I called Angela to get the address of the factory in the email Nick sent me and she said Nick needed me to get to the factory, that it was urgent. When you saw me tear out of here it was because I'd just hung up with her."

33

He sat up straight. "The same Angela who you found dead at Nick's showroom?"

"Yes. It doesn't make a lot of sense. He acted like he never asked her to call me. And there's something else."

He shook his head back and forth. "You didn't withhold evidence, did you?"

"Of course not! This next part is theory."

"Yeah, the cops don't want to hear theories," he said. See, we both learn from our mistakes.

"After Angela's body fell out of the sample closet, the phone rang. I thought maybe it was something about Nick's business, so I answered."

"And?"

"It was a guy. He made it sound like Angela's death was a message to Nick. And just that morning, Nick told Vito Cantone he wasn't going to do business with him. My first thought was that Vito killed Angela. Especially after Loncar told us Angela used to date him."

"Could he have done it? Was there time?"

"I don't know. It would have been tight, but maybe she knew Vito was headed out to Nick and wanted to warn him."

"But something else is bothering you."

"The caller referred to Nick as my boyfriend, and Vito knew Nick and I were engaged. Nick told him when we were at the factory." I leaned back and gave full consideration to the one question that had lingered since I'd spoken to Loncar. "What if there's something else Nick is hiding that led to Angela's murder?"

6

NICKY'S GIRL

*E*ddie sat back and laced his fingers behind his head. His blond hair was a whiter shade than usual thanks to an overly zealous application of peroxide. His usual rock band T-shirt had been temporarily replaced with a black one with the words, "Do or do not. There is no try."

"You think Nick is keeping something from you?" he asked.

"I don't know. He's acting a little funny. Not funny-funny, but peculiar-funny."

"How so?" He put a hand out in front of him. "Wait. If it has to do with your sex life, I don't want to hear it."

Last month, Eddie and Cat (of the had-a-baby-and-moved-to-Philly fame), had accused me of not opening up and sharing details of my personal life. A little more than I think they'd bargained for came out of that discussion, and since then, I'd make a concerted effort to confide in them.

"It doesn't have to do with my sex life, but I don't have anything concrete. It's like—he's always been so *there*, you know? When I was freaking out when I first moved to Ribbon, he was this solid pillar of strength, even while I thought he was a bad guy. And then after that was over, there was that thing with the knockoff handbag ring and

35

he helped me. Even through the break up and the Dante days, he was—I don't know—*there*. But ever since the engagement, even before I found Angela, it's like he's been drifting away."

"What about his dad? Does Nick act the same around him?"

"I don't know. I haven't been to their house in a couple of days."

He slapped his knees and stood up. "It's probably all in your head. The guy just asked you to marry him. Maybe reality sunk in and he's starting to realize what life with you is going to be like."

I picked up my empty coffee cup and threw it at Eddie. He caught it, tossed it into the trash can, and left. The memory of his laughter remained long after the sound of it faded down the corridor.

I spent the morning outlining the costs and tasks involved in my photo shoot and the afternoon working on the concept boards. Rex Andrew Garvin, the manager of the store's shipping and receiving department, stopped by after lunch. He was a forty-year-old black man with wire framed glasses, a black polo shirt, and jeans. An external back support was Velcroed around his waist and he had two work gloves bunched up in his left hand. Despite his overly formal name (or perhaps in light of it), everybody in the store called him Ragu. The nickname was probably inspired by his initials, but maybe also encouraged by his habit of bringing canned spaghetti for lunch.

"Hey, Samantha," he said. "I heard you might need my department to deliver some samples to a photo shoot."

I pushed aside the concept boards. "I was going to call you. How did you hear that already?"

"The ops manager told me. Must have come from the weekly senior manager's meeting. Did I hear wrong?"

"No, you heard right."

He came into the office and looked at the mess of papers, printed images from runway shows, and glue sticks on my desk. "Is this how your office always looks?"

"No. I'm getting caught up after vacation."

"You woulda made a good Kindergarten teacher."

I hardly thought a messy desk and ownership of more than one glue stick were endorsements for the care and early education responsibilities of small children but kept that thought to myself. To Ragu, I said, "I don't have details yet, but I'm hoping to set something up by the end of the week."

"Cool. Give me a day notice and I'll take care of it. How big of a truck will you need?"

"It depends on how many samples the buyers are able to get on short notice, but I think the store van should be fine."

"Cool," he said again. He glanced at my desk again. "Keep me posted." He turned and left.

By five thirty I had lined up three potential factories for the shoot and an appointment schedule to start scouting them in the morning. I sent an email to the senior management team letting them know I wouldn't be in until noon.

As I waited for a response, I opened a search window and typed in the name "Angela di Sotto." The top link went to Angela's obituary in the online edition of the *Ribbon Times*. It was short: no cause of death, no police statement, no mention of her mafia ties. The last line of the article said she'd been outlived by her half-sister, Connie di Sotto, and provided an address for flowers and gifts.

I copied the address down and collected my coat and bag. On my way out of the office, I ran into Pam Trotter with her assistant, Wanda.

"Samantha, how are things with the photo shoot?" Pam asked.

"So far, so good. I'm scouting factories tomorrow morning. The concept boards are sitting on Nancie's desk and I've worked up a preliminary budget. Have the buyers had any luck securing the samples?"

"We're in luck. Most retailers aren't doing their shoots until next month, so we were able to get runway samples overnighted. They should be here tomorrow. Our problem is going to be the shoes."

Wanda looked at me funny. "Can't you just get them from Nick?" she asked.

Pam looked from Wanda to me. "Nick...Nick Taylor? That's right, you two have a history, don't you?"

"Yes," I said. I hiked my bag up onto my shoulder and Wanda pointed at my hand.

"Oh my gosh, are you and Nick engaged? You're getting married? Nick's getting married? What a pretty ring! Is it vintage?" The more animated Wanda got, the more people around us stopped to take notice of who was getting engaged to Nick Taylor.

Heat climbed my neck. Wanda grabbed my hand and pulled it close to her. I looked from her to Pam, who smiled. I rolled my eyes and she nodded her head. I relaxed and let Wanda have her moment (my moment) and then pulled my hand back and slipped on my gloves. The leather bunched up over the ring, leaving a lump.

"I haven't had a chance to ask Nick about the samples, not after what happened at his showroom yesterday," I said.

Pam put her hand on my forearm. "If he can do it, great. It'll be nice exposure for him, which might help offset any negative press he'll get now. And if he can't do it, we'll reach out to one of the designers who keeps basic inventory on hand or we'll use something generic from the sample closet."

I'd been so busy worrying about asking Nick for a favor that I hadn't stopped to think about the potential benefits to him. If he could get us samples direct from Italy, his shoes would be featured exclusively in our spread in the first catalog of the season, plus would be shown in the *Ribbon Times* interview that Carl Collins was putting together. It would be wrong for me *not* to ask him.

I left Pam and Wanda by the store exit and ran to my car. The early January temperature reminded me that winter was here and wasn't planning on leaving for a while. I started the engine and rubbed my arms with my hands. Cold wisps of air crept into where the convertible's hard top attached to the car. It was better than a traditional soft top convertible, but not much.

I drove to Nick's showroom. The door remained taped shut, and the interior was dark. A cluster of cars were parked in the lot. People stood on the sidewalk, pressing their faces up to the window that had separated Nick and me the day before, likely destroying the residual palm prints from where we'd placed our hands on opposite sides of the glass. I drove past them and parked outside of the grocery store at the end of the lot.

Last month, when Cat's husband had been murdered, she'd received a refrigerator filled with casseroles from neighbors, coworkers, and just about anybody who stopped by to offer condolences. I didn't trust my culinary skills enough to test tonight and didn't think my go-to meal of Brother's Pizza was appropriate to take to a grieving family, so I did the next best thing. I went into the grocery store and bought the largest frozen lasagna they carried, and asked Siri directions to Angela di Sotto's address.

The di Sotto family lived about five miles west of Tradava, almost all on the highway. My stop off at the grocery store had delayed my trip slightly, but traffic was light thanks to people prolonging their holiday vacations. Once I exited the highway, I doubled back along a side street. Even without Siri's help, I would have easily picked out which house was my destination; a driveway filled with shiny luxury cars and a florist's van were parked in front of a large white brick mansion.

There was a very large chance my frozen lasagna would be underwhelming.

I convinced myself that stopping by with my version of a condolence casserole was more about the gesture than the actual item and climbed out of the car. The wind snapped at my legs. I tightened my pashmina scarf around my neck and approached the front of the house. I rang the bell. A series of chimes announced me on the other side of the door. I adjusted the lasagna box against my hip and shifted my weight from foot to foot.

The door opened and an Italian woman with glamorously streaked gray and white hair faced me. She was in her mid-fifties, dressed in a red leopard printed V-neck sweater and tight black pants. Gold hoop earrings swung from her ears, and a gold chain with a teardrop-shaped pendant hung around her neck. Her lips were dark cherry red.

"Come in, you poor thing, you're gonna freeze if you just keep standing out there." She held the door open and waved me in with her spare hand.

"Hi," I said. "I'm Samantha Kidd. I came by to pay my respects to Angela's family." As soon as the door was shut behind me, I was enveloped in a cloud of meatballs and marinara with a side note of Opium perfume.

"I'm her half-sister, Connie di Sotto. Come on in."

"I'm so sorry for your loss." I held the frozen lasagna awkwardly, wondering if I could hide it under my coat without her noticing.

She glanced at the box and her mouth turned down on both sides. Her expression told me everything I'd feared. She didn't take the lasagna, but now that she'd noticed it, there was no avoiding my gaffe.

"This is for you," I said. "I'm—I'm not the best cook."

She took the box. "How did you know Angela?"

"I knew her from her job with Nick Taylor. I'm his—" I paused. I was still getting used to the word. "I'm his fiancé."

Connie's expression changed so quickly that for a moment I wondered if someone had pulled a string behind her head. "You're Nicky's girl? Come meet the ladies!"

She walked away from me toward the yummy scent. That's odd, I thought. Last night Nick acted like he didn't know Angela's family. Curiosity forced me to follow her.

We reached the kitchen. Two women in varying shades of animal prints sat around a wooden table. A card game was in play. A very short older woman stood by the stove behind them moving a silver ladle back and forth between several large pots. If I'd been expecting a quiet group of mourners, I would have been disappointed. Not having much experience in paying respects to families of the recently deceased, I hadn't expected anything.

Connie tossed my frozen lasagna onto the counter. "Look who came by. Nicky's girl!"

The women dropped their cards and introduced themselves. "I'm Debbi Blum," said the platinum blonde wearing a bright pink leopard printed sweatshirt.

"I'm Katie Caprero," said the redheaded woman in the green tiger stripe.

All three women started talking. "Take off your coat! Sit down!

Can I get you something? Glass of Lambrusco?" Their voices overlapped, and I had a hard time keeping up with who said what.

I held my hands up. "No thank you. I just came by to—" I glanced at the lasagna quickly and then looked back at Connie. "I wanted to say how sorry I am for what happened to Angela. It has to be hard losing a family member."

"It is," Connie said. The women at the table exchanged looks amongst themselves but didn't speak. Connie lowered her gaze and stared at something inconsequential. The room fell silent for a moment.

"*Basta!*" exclaimed the small woman by the stove. "Angela was never part of this family." She threw the sauce-covered ladle onto the white counter, splattering marinara on the surrounding surfaces. She untied her apron, threw it onto the floor, and stormed out of the room, leaving the rest of us stunned into silence.

7

THE ANIMAL PRINT BRIGADE

"*M*ama!" Debbi, the woman in pink leopard print, called out. She jumped up and chased after the woman and left me alone in the kitchen with the other animal prints.

"Don't mind her none," said Connie. "That's Mama Blum. She's Debbi's mom, my aunt. When Angela's mother died, Mama Blum and Debbi raised her. Angela was always a wild child. Mama said Debbi had to learn to control her before something bad would happen."

Katie spoke up. "Yeah, it's a tragedy, but it's not a surprise. We all thought Nicky was a doll for giving her a job."

"How do you all know Nick?" I asked.

Katie smiled. "When Nicky hired Angela, he became part of the family. Now he's getting married. I can't believe Angela didn't say anything. Another one bites the dust, ladies," she said to Connie, who chuckled.

"It's not—it wasn't her fault. It just happened over Christmas. I don't even know if Nick had a chance to tell her."

"Don't you worry, honey, we'll make sure you feel like part of the family too. As soon as this thing with Angela dies down."

They weren't exactly heartbroken over Angela's murder. Was this just another way people grieved? I was here to pay my respects, but the longer I stood awkwardly in the middle of the kitchen, the more I felt like they weren't treating her death as a tragedy. They were treating it like a matter of fact—no more consideration than a burnt pizza crust.

Chimes from the grandfather clock in the hallway rang out. What was that—seven? The last time Nick and I had spoken, I'd told him to expect me for dinner. Even if I went straight to his apartment, I wouldn't arrive until close to seven thirty.

"Come have a seat and tell us all about yourself," Katie said.

"I'm sorry, I can't stay. I didn't realize how late it was, and I just wanted to drop off the lasagna." The women looked at my empty hands, which I quickly moved into my coat pockets. "It was lovely meeting you all. I'll let myself out."

Thanks to a combination of green lights and daredevil driving, I pulled into Nick's parking garage fourteen minutes later. I hung my visitor pass on the rearview mirror and ran into the building. Nick answered my knock on the door almost immediately.

He kissed me hello. "When are you going to learn you don't have to knock?"

"I think it's best that I knock. I don't need to walk in on you and your dad sitting around in your underwear watching football."

He crossed his arms. A moment later, he held out his hand. "Hi. I'm Nick Taylor. I don't believe we've met."

I swatted his hand out of the way. "You know what I mean. Give me a chance to discover your annoying habits over time."

"My life is an open book, Kidd. You should know that better than anybody."

I had always thought so, but after today I wasn't so sure. I followed him into the living room trying to figure out a way to ask him about the animal print brigade. Despite the heat, the outside chill had left me shivering. I stayed bundled in my coat and sat on the corner of the sofa.

Nick Senior sat in his recliner. He was a seventy-year-old bald man recovering from a hip injury. His brown eyes held the same sparkle that he'd passed down to Nick. "You're late," he said.

"I know. I'm sorry. I went to Angela di Sotto's house after work to pay my respects to her family. I thought it would be nice to drop off some food."

"You took food to the di Sotto house," Nick said. It was more of a statement than a question.

"That's what people do, right? I'm trying to be normal. Samantha 2.0." Whoops, Nick didn't know about the new and improved Samantha 2.0. He raised an eyebrow. "I mean, it was the right thing. I knew her through you, and it was a gesture."

"What'd you take them, a pizza?" Nick's dad asked. Ever since moving in with Nick, his dad had gotten to know me all too well.

"No, I didn't take them a pizza," I said like I was insulted by the thought. The two men waited for me to continue. "I took them a lasagna."

Nick Senior laughed out loud. "You were wearing that coat? They must have thought you were a relief worker." He got up and walked into the kitchen for a beer.

"Samantha 2.0?" Nick asked.

"Forget about that. Something's been bothering me, and I need to ask you about it." I pulled my pashmina scarf from around my neck and shrugged out of my coat. Nick took the garments and tossed them onto a chair by the dining room table. "Why aren't people grieving over Angela's murder?"

"People grieve in different ways."

"Yes, but her family was sitting around the kitchen playing cards and drinking Lambrusco. Your dad is cracking jokes about my lasagna. Even you—"

He put his finger up to my lips. "I sent flowers this morning and made a donation in Angela's name to St. Catherine of Siena Sisters of Mercy. I spent my morning at the police station telling Loncar everything I knew about her in the hopes that he can find who did this."

"But are you upset? Did you cry or eat ice cream? Do you want to get a cat? They help."

"Kidd, I'm not like you. You want me to talk about it, but that's not me."

"But you are processing her loss, right? You're not talking, you're not freaking out, you're not stress eating. It doesn't seem normal. We're supposed to be planning a life together, so I should know how you deal with tragedy. I just need to know you're not a machine."

He reached his hand out and stroked the side of my face with the back of his knuckles. "I tend to bottle things up. I probably learned it from watching my dad try to be strong after my mom died. I'm not used to having someone call me on it."

Nick Senior dad came back to the living room, the laughter at my expense still visible on his face. "You took her a lasagna. It was frozen, wasn't it? Tell me it was frozen." I didn't say anything. "This is priceless. Junior, this one's a keeper. Life won't get boring with her." He sat down and picked up the remote.

"Dad, Samantha and I need a minute."

"You can talk in the kitchen. That's the room that *doesn't* have a TV."

Nick took my hand and led me to the kitchen. He poured two glasses of red wine and handed me one. "I don't know how to process what happened to Angela except to talk to the police and hope they find the person who did this. Kidd, I know how you are, and I think it was very sweet of you to take something to Angela's house today, but I want that to be it, okay? I want you to stay out of Loncar's investigation."

"What if you're in trouble?"

He diverted his eyes. Again, the mask of control slipped into place and hid his emotions.

I put my hands on his arms and stepped closer to him. "Don't shut me out. Please. If you *are* in trouble, tell me. I can help you."

Before he had a chance to answer, his dad came back into the kitchen. "You don't see me, you don't hear me. I'm not here. Just need some towels to mop up the spilled beer."

Nick ignored his dad and continued. "This whole thing scares me, Kidd. I don't want you to get involved. There are plenty of factories around Ribbon. If Vito wants to negotiate, he can talk to me. I won't let him use you to manipulate my decision."

Nick Senior stopped. "Vito? Vito Cantone? Haven't heard that name in a long time. Why are you talking to him?" He waited for a response from Nick, one hand filled with a wad of paper towels and no urgency to put them to use.

When Nick didn't answer, I did. "He wants Nick to rent out a factory in Ribbon. Nick said no. I was going to use the factory myself, but Nick doesn't want me to."

Nick Senior's expression lost its sparkle and he looked back and forth between me and his son. "You two better figure this thing out. Lots of potential for conflicts of interest." He tucked the rest of the roll of paper towels under his arm and left us alone again.

We stood in the kitchen facing each other. Pam's suggestion that I ask Nick about the shoes for the photo shoot popped into my head, but that wasn't keeping our work and personal lives separate, that was weaving them together like threads on a loom. I thought again about how Nancie was leaving the company she started to go work with her fiancé in New Mexico, and if that was the only option that would work: either Nick or I choosing a career and the other one stepping into the role of supportive spouse.

The wall-mounted phone rang. I was so startled by the unexpected sound that I jumped.

Nick answered. "This is Nick Taylor," he said. "No, I've been working from home ever since I left you. Why?" He turned his back to me, listened for a moment, and then said, "I'll be right there." He slammed the plastic phone back onto the wall mount. The base cracked with the impact. "Get your coat. We're going to my showroom."

"Why?"

"You want to be in the loop, right?"

"Um, right. I think so. What happened? Who was that?"

"That was Detective Loncar. He said somebody threw a slab of cement into my showroom window."

8

CHOPPED LIVER

We arrived at the showroom quickly. The entire front glass window had been smashed, and a large, round chunk of cement sat inside. Two of the pedestals that displayed shoe samples had been knocked over and now lay broken and bent on the floor. A team of men dressed in jeans and black hooded sweatshirts stood with Loncar. Thick suede work gloves and dusty work boots completed their look.

"Mr. Taylor," Loncar said. "I didn't expect you to bring Ms. Kidd."

"I was with him when you called," I said by way of explaining my presence. "What happened here?"

Loncar looked at me for a few seconds, and then turned to Nick. "We got a call from the sandwich shop two doors down. Said he saw a white van drive past the store, and then a few seconds later he heard a crash. By the time he got out to the sidewalk, the van was too far away for him to get the plates. He saw the broken glass and called us."

"What is that?" I asked.

"Appears to be the base of one of the streetlamps." Loncar looked out into the parking lot and Nick and I followed his gaze. He was right. The lamps that had been spaced throughout the parking lot were cemented into place in large, round concrete bases.

"How much does something like that weight?" I asked.

"More than you'd think."

I looked at Nick. He was angry, and I didn't blame him. If this had been a prank, it was far from funny. The problem was, I was pretty sure it hadn't been a prank. "Detective, was the store still sealed?"

Loncar nodded. "We don't know if the cement through the glass was the crime, or if it was the means to commit a different crime inside. At this point, the interior has been compromised. I need you to go inside and tell me if anything looks out of place. Can you do that?"

"Sure." Nick pulled his keys out of his pocket and went to the door.

"Um, Nick?" I pointed to the broken window.

"I pay good money to have a door and a lock and a key. I'm using them."

Loncar pulled a pocket knife out of his jacket and pierced the tape that sealed the entrance. He slid it around the perimeter of the door and then stood back and nodded at Nick. Nick unlocked the door and stepped inside.

"You wait out here with me," Loncar said to me.

"Fine."

We stood on the sidewalk while Nick walked around the show-room. He glanced at Angela's desk, fanned a couple of folders across the surface, and then left them and disappeared into the back by his office. I hopped from foot to foot, trying to stay warm. Loncar kept his hands shoved in the pocket of his coat.

"Things good with you two?" Loncar asked.

"We got engaged over Christmas."

"Congratulations."

"How are things with your wife?" I asked.

"We're talking." He stared ahead at the showroom even though Nick was nowhere to be seen. "I met my granddaughter for the first time last night."

"That's great!" The officers on the sidewalk turned toward us. I lowered my voice. "That's great," I said again, this time much quieter.

"Man, she's cute. That little baby. She's got these little fists. She just balls 'em up and wipes her face with them."

"Logan does that when he's cleaning himself." The detective glanced at me. "I don't have a lot of experience with actual babies. Cats are more my speed."

"You two ever talk about that? Whether you want kids?"

"Who, me and Nick?"

"Are you engaged to anybody else?"

"No. Um, no. I figure one step at a time."

"Don't wait too long. Deal breakers like that should be out in the open up front."

I let Loncar's comment go unanswered and turned my attention back toward the store. Random passersby were angling for a view of the action. The officers present kept busy by ushering them farther down the parking lot. I imagined the businesses at both ends of the strip mall would see a boost in business tonight. A little too late for the video store that had posted a Going Out of Business sign the day after Christmas but good for the grocery store where I'd bought the frozen lasagna.

I pointed at the chunk of cement inside Nick's store. "Where do you get something like that?" I asked.

"Dump site, concrete factory, landfill, who knows. Could be it was stolen from a public area."

"But a chunk of cement that big—what would that weigh?"

"Four, five hundred pounds."

"A van drives into a populated strip mall during regular hours, some guys throw a five-hundred-pound block of cement through Nick's showroom window and drive off. Nobody saw anything. How does that happen? There are always people around here. It's one of the reasons Nick rented space in this strip mall. There's plenty of parking, it's not far from the buying offices of Tradava. That other big department store was supposed to move in and he would have had proximity to them too."

"Ms. Kidd, I know you're a smart lady so I'm going to be frank with you. I'm not telling you anything that won't show up in tomorrow's paper. This does not appear to be a random act of vandalism. On the heels of a murder at this very same location, after we sealed off the store so the evidence would not be contaminated, this is a message. If there were witnesses, they don't want to come forward. But somebody with the means to pull off both of those acts has taken an interest in Mr. Taylor's business."

"Nick's going to die, isn't he?" My eyes widened to stave off impending tears. I was suddenly aware of my heart thumping in my chest, driving an aggressive flow of adrenaline to my extremities. "They're going to come after him next. There has to be something I can do."

"This is a police matter."

"Don't tell me to stay out of it," I told Loncar. "I'm not going to let him handle this himself."

"What am I, chopped liver?"

Loncar's possible attempt to lighten the mood was interrupted by Nick coming out of the showroom. Once again, he ignored the exit provided by the broken glass and left through the door.

"I think I know what this was about," Nick said. He looked back and forth between our faces, probably anticipating Loncar's request that I go stand by myself in a corner somewhere while they talked. I think we were both surprised when that instruction never came.

"What'd you find?" Loncar asked.

"It's what I didn't find," Nick said. His breath came out in puffs of condensation. He blew on his hands and rubbed them against each other. "Somebody went through the file cabinets where I keep the personnel records. Most are in there on the floor." He paused, looked back at the showroom, and then refocused on Loncar. "Angela's file is gone."

9

OBSTRUCTION OF JUSTICE

"What else was stolen?" I asked. Loncar shot me a look that said he was running the investigation, not me. "Oh, come on. It's not like you weren't about to ask the same thing."

"It's too soon to tell," Nick said. "Everything I need to run the business is backed up on the cloud. I make my sketches by hand and the sketch pads for the last five seasons are in the cabinet where I keep previous season information."

"You're saying the only thing stolen was Angela di Sotto's file?"

"Looks that way."

"Wait a minute," I said. "Why wasn't Angela's resume on your computer? How'd she apply for the job?"

"She was a walk-in. Said she saw my job posting on a message board at her continuing education program."

"She just showed up and you hired her?" The tiniest part of me was jealous, but not for the obvious reasons.

I'd spent the past two years looking for work in Ribbon and had come with nine years of experience from a major New York retailer. To think that Angela had shown up, resume in hand, and talked her way into a primo job as showroom manager for a high profile designer label under any other circumstances would have engendered envy.

The two men looked at me. "What? We all know I've had troubled employment. Maybe I just want to know what to try in case this whole Tradava thing doesn't work out."

"Angela introduced herself and said she'd spent the past two years going to night school for her degree in small business management. She grew up in the garment industry and had a knowledge of how to calculate markup, landing costs, and general retail math. She was frustrated by trying to find a job online. She had a folder filled with positive endorsements and letters of recommendation from former employers and professors. And, not to sound superficial, but she looked the part."

"And you needed a showroom manager," I said.

"And I needed a showroom manager," Nick repeated.

Loncar jotted some notes in the small spiral bound notebook he carried around with him. "Mr. Taylor, I know I don't need to tell you this, but your showroom is still off-limits. We're going to get a team out here to secure the place in a way that will keep everybody out, and that includes you." He looked at me and I crossed my arms over my chest. "If there's anything you need to run your business from home, I suggest you get it now. Give me a list of whatever you take, and one of my guys will get photographs so there's no confusion."

Nick looked back at the showroom. "I was supposed to leave for Italy at the end of the week. There's no way I can get on that plane now. I'm going to lose my production window at the factory and probably an entire season of delivery. I might never recover financially."

As soon as Nick said the word "factory," I flashed back to yesterday morning. Had it only been a day and a half since we'd met with Vito on Canal Street? Was it possible Nick's refusal to do business with Vito had led to a murder and an act of vandalism so egregious it could cost Nick his company?

Nick went back inside the showroom. Loncar turned to me. "What?" he asked.

"What what?"

"You reacted to something he said. I want to know what it was."

"It was nothing. Okay, it wasn't nothing, but it wasn't something, either. I was just wondering if this had anything to do with Nick telling Vito he didn't want to use his factory yesterday morning, but I have nothing to connect those two things. No facts. You work on facts. If I'm wrong, you're going to waste valuable time investigating a fake lead." I bit my lower lip and tried not to say anything else. The effort failed. "This is what you wanted, right? For me to be a law-abiding citizen who stays out of your investigations? This is what that looks like. Me. Standing here. Not telling you things I can't prove."

"Ms. Kidd, the second that theory of yours turns into fact, I want to know. Because if I find out you're holding back on information that can lead to a mob arrest in my back yard, I'm going to arrest you myself for obstruction of justice."

"Detective, if I had evidence of the mob in our back yard, I would tell you. Until yesterday I didn't even know there *was* mob in our back yard. See? You're already one step ahead of me."

Nick came back with a sketchpad under his arm. Loncar directed one of his officers to take pictures of the pages inside and Nick complied. It had been a long day and a long night, and I didn't know how Nick was still standing because I was about to collapse from hunger.

We left the police to secure the storefront. Instead of getting onto the highway, Nick turned left out and in about a quarter mile turned right into the parking lot of the Tradava strip mall.

"You never got dinner. I'll buy you a pizza," he said.

"You don't have to do that."

"Kidd, you've been great through this whole thing. Calm and rational and asking all the right questions. Thank you."

"You don't have to thank me."

"Yes, I do. There's been more than one time in the past when you did this exact same thing and I told you not to get involved. And here it is. It's me bringing trouble into your life." He parked in a space not far from Brother's Pizza and turned off the engine.

"Will your business survive this?"

"I don't know. Probably. Maybe. Maybe not."

After Nick had taken the business over from his dad, he'd licensed his name for financial backing. A couple of years ago, he reclaimed ownership of all aspects of the company. It had been a slow build from there. Instead of his shoes being in every major high end retailer, scaling back production had meant his accounts were cherry-picked. Tradava was one of them. He'd never told me his debt to income ratio, but I'd assumed his company was healthy. Maybe I'd been wrong.

"When I bought back distribution of my label, I put everything I had into the company. This is my make-it-or-break-it year. I thought things were on the right track, but they're not." He studied me. "That wasn't the life I wanted to offer you when I asked you to marry me."

"Is that why you've been different since I said yes? I thought you had second thoughts."

"No—don't ever think that. Okay?"

The relationship fears I'd felt yesterday morning bubbled below the surface. I knew Nick didn't expect me to give up my world for him, but I could tell his sudden lack of footing in his world caused him to question bigger issues. We needed to talk about what this meant.

"Me saying yes was never about you offering me a life," I said. "It was about you offering me a commitment and a companion. I already have a life. I thought it would be nice to share it with you— no matter what happens."

He smiled. "Come on. Let's get you that pizza."

I opened my door and climbed out. A man in a streaked white apron came out of Brothers and looked our way. I recognized him as Jimmy, one of the two brothers who hand-tossed my pizzas in high school and had since inherited the shop from their dad. It was late and not terribly busy, and I assumed he had arranged for someone else to lock up so he could cut out early.

I shut my door and met Nick around the back of the truck. "Hey, Jimmy," I called out. "You're not closing early, are you?"

Jimmy didn't answer me. He strode right up to Nick and punched him in the face.

10

ROCKY BALBOA

The punch clipped Nick's cheek. His head whipped to the side and he put his hands out onto the back of his truck to keep his balance. He balled up his fists and answered Jimmy's punch with an uppercut. Jimmy's head snapped back, and he swung again. Nick ducked. He put his hand on his cheek and faced Jimmy. The two men circled each other, shoulders hunched, elbows bent, hands fisted.

"Get outta here," Jimmy said. "We don't need your business." He looked at me. I was pretty sure my pizza habit had paid for their recent renovation. He pointed at Nick. "You back with this guy?"

I nodded.

"I liked the other one better." He spit on the ground by Nick's back tires, glared at Nick, and then walked away.

Nick pulled off his glove and held his hand to his face. "Was that about you?"

"Me? No. How could it have to do with me? I'm his best customer."

"Here," he said. He pulled out his wallet and handed me a twenty. "I'll wait in the truck."

"I don't need a pizza that bad. Put that away and let's get out of here."

Even though my car was still parked at Nick's, my house was less than a mile from the Brother's parking lot. Considering the evening we'd had, it was the logical destination. Nick pulled his truck into the garage and we went inside.

"Are you hungry?" I asked.

"No. You eat."

"How about ice for your eye?"

"I don't need ice. I need a shower." He went upstairs.

He was avoiding me and the questions I felt sure he knew I wanted to ask. I went into the kitchen. I slathered some butter on a piece of bread and ate it while standing up. Logan joined me, and I tore off a second piece and put it in his bowl.

It had been an evening of surprises, starting with the vandalism and ending with the fight.

I'd never seen Nick fight. I'd hardly ever seen him mad. Sure, there were a few moments where his anger had been right below the surface, but that was normal for everybody. Tonight was different.

For someone who appeared to be in control of his life and his business, he'd been pushed to his limits. I couldn't imagine what made Jimmy punch him, but I understood why Nick had punched back. He was defending himself, not against a pizza store owner, but against unknown forces that were trying to knock him down. Jimmy had simply put a face on the situation. But the question remained: why in the name of all the cheesy goodness that came from a 500-degree pizza oven would Jimmy slug Nick?

I put away the bread and loaded the dishwasher. The water upstairs turned off. It was going on eleven and I had to get up early for work the next day. I climbed the stairs and went into the bedroom to change into pajamas. The bathroom door opened, and Nick came out. He was bare-chested, a towel wrapped around his waist, another towel draped around his neck. His curly brown hair was shiny with moisture.

"You look like Rocky Balboa," I said. I reached up and traced my fingers over the bruise that was forming under his eye. "Does it hurt?"

His eyes grew dark and he leaned down and kissed me. My hand was still on his cheek. His kiss turned into a nip of my lower lip, and then a longer kiss. His hands reached to my navy knit dress and felt over the parts of me where the fabric clung the most. I moved my hands up onto his wet hair and he pulled my dress off over my head.

This was unexpected.

We advanced from standing to laying, from kissing to—well, that's none of your business—and soon, our energy spent, we both lay back on the bed. I arranged the covers over us and rested against my pillow. The last words Nick had spoken were, "I need a shower." While our few dalliances thus far had left no evidence that he was a dirty talker, I wouldn't have minded a phrase or two after the fact to let me know what he was thinking.

I removed my nightgown from under my pillow (habit from childhood) and slipped it over my head. Nick pulled on his boxers and undershirt. He lay back and pulled me into a half embrace. In a whisper that was almost inaudible, he said, "I don't know what I'd do without you, Kidd." He pressed his lips against the side of my head. I rested my arm across his chest, closed my eyes, and fell asleep moments later.

I woke up alone. I'd left my phone in my handbag in the living room and had no idea what time it was. I pulled a red zip-front hoodie over my nightgown and went downstairs. Nick was in the kitchen making breakfast. He wore the jeans he'd had on last night and his white undershirt. The bruise on his cheek had turned purple and a greenish-yellow shade discolored the tender area directly under his eye. It was oddly sexy, a fact that I kept to myself.

"Good morning," he said. "I'm making you pancakes. Can you handle that? I know it's not your normal Pop-Tart breakfast of champions."

"I didn't know I had pancake batter," I said.

"There was a box of Bisquick in the cupboard."

"I think my parents left that before they moved out."

Nick looked at the stack of pancakes he'd already made, pursed his lips as if considering the implications of using two-year-old dry goods, and shrugged. He handed me a plate and pointed me to the table. "I had some and I survived. You'll be fine. Sit. Eat. Then go get ready for work."

"My car is at your house."

"I'll drop you off. When I pick you up after work, I'll take you to my place and you can drive it home."

"But I need my car today."

"Why?"

I set the plate down and turned back to Nick. "I have a morning filled with appointments to check out factories for the photo shoot I pitched to Tradava. After you told me not to do business with Vito, I had to come up with a new plan."

"Kidd, I don't like it."

"I already got approval from Pam Trotter."

"That was before the murder and the vandalism."

"I can't just tell my boss that I'm not pursuing the project because my fiancé changed his mind." I searched his face and saw concern.

"You mentioned your project before, but you didn't tell me the details."

"Models in colorful tweed suits shot against the stark backdrop of a factory or warehouse. Juxtapose the glamour of ladylike dressing with the cold emptiness of exposed concrete and cement."

His body language relaxed and he smiled. "You're right. It's a good idea. But why the rush? The pre-fall catalog won't hit until July. You've got a couple of months to set this up."

"You know Carl Collins?"

"Everybody in Ribbon knows Carl. He's the town nuisance."

"He's been bugging me for an interview for the paper, something about Ribbon's Connie Blair or something. I've been blowing him off. But then I thought, if I could get him to do the interview with a staged version of the photo shoot in the background behind us, then Tradava would get extra exposure. They'd be the first catalog to showcase the fall trend, they could take advance orders on the merchandise, and if we style it with black tights, gloves, and sunglasses, we could probably get an uptick in sales on those categories now."

"What about the shoes?"

I hadn't had a chance to ask Nick about the shoe production, and with the new troubles from last night, I wasn't sure about the timing.

"The easiest thing to do would be to use whatever we have in the sample closet," I said.

"Sure," he said. "Or you could have asked me to order the samples."

"I was a shoe buyer, Nick. I know shoe samples cost about a thousand dollars each when you factor in the expense of the factory shutting down mass production to make one pair. I wasn't going to ask you to take a financial hit because I needed a favor. Not now."

"Okay, then think about this: if I don't have my factory produce *something*, then I'm going to lose my slot in the production calendar. Every other designer who uses that factory will get made before me and my spring collection will be produced in April. My order will ship in May and get marked down in June. There's no way my inventory will sell through in a month. I'll either pay a fortune in gross margin guarantees or take a loss when the retailers return their unsold inventory for credit on next season. I *know* you were a shoe buyer. None of this should be news to you."

I considered his side of things. "Either way you're screwed."

"No, either way it's my problem to figure out. Your problem is getting to those appointments and lining up a backdrop for your awesome photo shoot idea." He pulled his keys out of his pocket. "Take my truck. I'll meet you at the store when you're done, and we'll get your car. Deal?"

"What are you going to do all day?"

"Can I use your computer?"

"Sure."

"Good. Considering I have a black eye, I doubt I'll inspire a lot of confidence in person. I'll set up camp in your upstairs office and do what I can from here."

Tradava was less than a mile from my house, and if the temperature wasn't in the twenties, I might have let the voice inside my head convince me to offer to walk. (Even Samantha 2.0 had her limits.) I ate my pancakes, noticed no immediate side effects, and went upstairs. I took a quick shower and dressed in a blue jumpsuit and black Chelsea boots. I hooked two skinny black belts together and wound them around my waist, did a quick blow dry, kissed Nick good-bye, and left.

11

A MINEFIELD OF RELATIONSHIP PROBLEMS

hanks to the impromptu bedroom action last night, I'd forgotten to plug in my cell phone. I drove to Factory Row on Canal Street by memory, and then asked Siri to get me the final quarter mile. Driving Nick's white pick-up truck required a slight adjustment from how I drove my small convertible. I liked the perspective of being above most other cars, but the condition of the roads out this way were subpar, and by the time I arrived at the first factory, I was fairly certain I'd picked up some debris that was now stuck to the undercarriage.

The parking lot was empty. I climbed out of the truck and bent down to look underneath the truck. A plastic grocery store bag was stuck to a metal bar that connected the tires. I knew there was a name for that bar, but cars weren't my thing. I squatted and tried to knock the plastic bag loose, but it remained stuck. The parking lot was gravel and broken cement.

I took off my coat and tossed it down on the ground, and then sat on the lining and wriggled under the car with my legs sticking out. I grabbed the bag with both hands and it tore.

"Excuse me, this is a place of business. You can't work on your car here," said a female voice.

"Hold on, I'm almost done," I said. I gave the plastic one last yank. A round metal canister came loose and something dark dripped onto my face. Motor oil, I suspected.

"If you're not off this property in the next three minutes I'm calling the cops," the voice said.

I wiped the oil from my face and jammed the canister back into place. Slowly, I wriggled out from under the car. The peroxide-blond woman who stood in front of me was dressed in a brown leopard printed fake fur coat and black leather pants. By the time my eyes reached her face, recognition hit.

I stood up. "Debbi, right? Debbi Blum?" She nodded. "I'm Samantha Kidd. We met at Connie di Sotto's house. I came by yesterday to pay my respects to the family."

She made no effort to mask her surprise. She looked down my jumpsuit and raised both eyebrows, and then looked back up at my (probably oil-streaked) face. "Are you a mechanic? This is Nicky's truck, isn't it?"

"No. And yes. I work at Tradava. I borrowed Nick's truck today."

"You were trying to fix it? You know about cars?"

"I don't know anything about cars except I needed one to get to an appointment here."

"Wait a minute," she said. She held her index finger up, her long, red, square-cut fingernail moving back and forth as she moved her hand from side to side. "You're the person I'm meeting from Tradava?"

"I don't know. I'm meeting someone to talk about renting out a factory for a photo shoot."

"Yeah, that's me. It's my family's factory. You should've said something the other night. Follow me." She turned away.

I grabbed my coat from the ground and shook the gravel and cement bits from it, and then pulled it on and ran to catch up with her.

Unlike Vito Cantone's factory where I'd met up with Nick on Monday morning, Debbi's family's factory was in working order. Conveyor belts were set up like a maze throughout the interior.

Debbi flipped a large switch on the wall and light flooded the cavernous room.

"This factory is in use, isn't it?"

"Yeah," she said. "We're still closed for the holidays, but normally things get going around seven. Is that going to be a problem?"

"It might be."

"What do you need it for, anyway?"

I outlined my idea to Debbi. "To be honest, I was looking for something wide open and empty. The conveyor belts and machinery will probably be distracting in the background, and the focus is supposed to be on the clothes."

She glanced back at my jumpsuit. "You in fashion like Nicky?"

It took me a moment to realize what she was asking. "We used to work together. That's how we met—in New York. I was a buyer and he was a designer."

"He still is a designer. Aren't you a buyer no more?"

"No, I work on the store's catalog."

"That's probably better. Buyers have to keep up with fashion and your job is behind the scenes."

Clearly, she wasn't a fan of my jumpsuit.

"Besides," she continued. "Keep your lives separate, at least until after you're married."

"I think we'll try to keep our lives separate after we're married, too," I said.

She laughed. "Trust me. It's gonna be hard to keep your lives separate after you start having babies."

I wrapped my arms around my torso and kept quiet. I could only deal with so many issues at once.

Debbi and I walked out of the factory together. I fiddled with the seatbelt until after she pulled out of the lot and then got out and dumped a quart of oil into the place where the oil goes (I told you I don't know much about cars). I looked under the truck and didn't see anything drip.

I drove to the next factory on my schedule. It, too, was a fully functioning factory, and unlike Debbi's, had already returned to post-holiday production.

Over the sound of hydraulics and general machinery, I explained as best as I could that my factory needs were for backdrop, not production. The owner thanked me, and I left. By the time I arrived at the third factory, also in full swing, I knew there were two potential solutions: tell Tradava the idea wouldn't pan out, which would put my professional reputation in questionable light, or work out a deal with Vito.

But Angela was Vito's ex-girlfriend and she'd been killed. I'd be a fool not to see that choice as fraught with risk, danger, and a minefield of relationship problems.

I'd also be a fool not to see the opportunity to find out something more about Vito that might help Nick. He wasn't asking for my help but that didn't mean I wasn't going to give it.

Neither solution was ideal. Maybe Eddie would have a suggestion.

I climbed back into the truck and pulled out my phone. There were several missed calls from a number I didn't recognize, but no messages. I called Tradava and asked the operator to page Eddie for me. A few seconds later, he picked up. "Dude, where are you? You need to get here. Like five minutes ago."

"What's wrong? I'm scouting factories for the photo shoot. Don't tell me Tradava announced post-holiday layoffs. I can*not* handle getting laid off."

Eddie's voice dropped to a muffled whisper and I could barely make out what he said. "There are two women here who claim to be your friends. Katie Caprero and Connie di Sotto."

"They're at Tradava? In my office?"

"Yes. I can only entertain them for so long. Get here. Now."

12

THE TRADAVA BROTHERS

wo more of the leopard ladies were in my office?

"I'm on my way." I'd been so caught up on the phone that I hadn't stopped to notice a police car had pulled up behind Nick's truck. The sound of a siren went *Woop! Woop!* and his blue and red lights circled atop his cruiser.

"Is that the police? Were you arrested?" Eddie asked. In the background, I heard a woman's voice repeat the question.

"I wasn't arrested. I gotta go. I'll be there as soon as I can." I hung up and dropped the phone. The officer approached the driver's side window and I rolled it down and greeted him.

"Hi, I'm sorry. I know I'm not supposed to be on the shoulder of the road, but I got a call, and it was important, and I didn't think it was a good idea to talk on the phone and drive."

"License and registration, ma'am."

"Sure. But there's no trouble at all. I hung up, see?" I pointed to the phone on the floor. "And I'm on my way to work."

He didn't move. I pulled my license out of my wallet and then realized I didn't know where Nick kept his paperwork.

"Give me one second. This isn't my truck and I don't know where he keeps the registration." I opened the glove box and pulled out the owner's manual and service record books. The registration wasn't inside. "Hold on," I said, and flipped down the rearview mirror. The registration was clipped to the back and I handed it to the officer. "I borrowed the truck this morning. The owner gave me permission."

"Wait here," he said.

While the officer was running Nick's plates and my driving record, I retrieved the phone from the floor and called Nick. Words rushed out of me before he had a chance to speak. "I got pulled over," I said. "And your truck might be leaking oil and none of the factories are going to work except for Vito's and I know you don't want me to use it and if I don't, I'm afraid I'm going to lose my job."

"Kidd, slow down."

I leaned back against the driver's seat and inhaled sharply. The cold air speared my lungs. "It's been a big morning," I said.

"Tell me about it. Your friend the reporter showed up looking for you. Said he heard about my showroom over the wire and was mad because, apparently, you two have an arrangement? Should I be worried about this?"

"I don't know, Nick, should I be worried about the fact that a pizza store owner punched you last night?"

"Kidd—"

The officer returned to the truck window. "Hold on, here's the officer now." I held the phone out. "This is the truck owner. Do you want to talk to him?"

"No need. You're listed on his registration as co-owner of the truck."

"I am?" I put the phone back to my head. "I'm on your registration?"

"I thought it was a good idea. Finish up with the police and go to work. We'll straighten out everything later."

"Okay." I hung up. "When did he list me on his registration?"

"Couple of days ago. You work for Mr. Taylor?"

"No. We're engaged."

"That explains it. Usually these things happen when you get a job or get married. Bank account's probably next."

I sure hoped not. Nick didn't need to know how much I spent on pretzels.

The officer handed the paperwork back to me. "Just a warning this time. The shoulder of the highway is for emergencies. You best be on your way."

"Thank you, officer." I tucked the registration back under the visor and put my license in my wallet. Seconds later, I pulled off the shoulder.

I drove to Tradava and parked around back. Despite new shipments in three of my four favorite departments, I went straight to my office. Connie di Sotto sat at Nancie's empty desk and Katie Caprero sat at mine. Both ladies wore floor length fur coats. Connie's was black mink. Katie's was dark green that set off her auburn hair. Eddie sat in the chair in front of my desk with a look of panic on his face.

"Dude!" He jumped up. "Great, you're here. I have to get back to the store." He opened his eyes wide, shook his head, and then left.

I pushed aside every crisis that was jockeying for my attention and hugged them one at a time. "Connie, Katie. What are you doing here?"

Connie answered. "We heard about Nicky's showroom last night, poor thing. He's had a rough time of it lately so we started thinking how we could help, and Katie had an idea."

"We'll throw a benefit!" Katie said. She gestured widely with her hands and her fur coat opened to reveal a green leather blazer and leopard printed skirt. "Now, we don't have a ton of time, so we had to come here right away to get you involved."

"Can you believe none of us has your phone number?" Connie asked.

"You're right. That's a major oversight," I said. I unbuttoned my coat and slipped it off.

Connie's eyes dropped to my jumpsuit. "Were you working on a car?"

68

Again with the jumpsuit? "Yes," I said. "This jumpsuit is French. I bought it at a designer sample sale last month."

"Okay..." her voice trailed off. She didn't seem to believe me. "Debbi's out getting us a location. Mama sent the boys shopping. We're going to spend the afternoon telling everybody we know, and we'll open the doors tomorrow night. Can you come with?"

"Right now?"

"Yeah," she said. "Is that a problem?"

Before I could answer, Pam Trotter came around the corner with two older men. I recognized the one to her left from the picture that hung in the employee entrance. He was Harry Tradava, the owner of the store for which I currently worked. The other man was a slightly younger version of him.

"Samantha," Pam said. "Am I interrupting a meeting?"

"No, I was just finishing up." I picked up a business card from the edge of my desk, turned back to Connie and Katie. I flipped it over and scribbled my cell phone number on the back. "You two go on and call me later."

"Sure," Connie said. She took the card and flapped it back and forth past her cheek like a miniature fan. "Come on, Katie. We got work to do." She paused next to Pam and looked down at her feet. "Nice shoes," she said, and then left. Katie followed.

Pam waited for the outer door of the advertising wing to close and then turned back to me. "Friends of yours?"

"More like acquaintances. They're helping me find a factory for the photo shoot."

"That's exactly why we're here. Samantha, this is Harry Tradava and his brother, Otto. They're the co-owners of the company."

"I recognize your picture from the back hallway," I said to Harry, and shook his hand. I shook Otto's next. I tipped my head toward Harry, "*Older* brother, right?"

Otto smiled. "Ah. You understand." We all chuckled.

"Samantha, the Tradava brothers came by to visit the store and when I told them about you and your proposal, they insisted they meet you."

Harry spoke up. "I've read about you in the papers. Glad we were smart enough to put you on our payroll."

"I was sort of on your payroll when I first moved here," I said, "but things didn't quite work out."

Otto chimed in. "That's right. Patrick hired you, didn't he? Good man, Patrick. Did a lot for the reputation of our store. Too bad, what happened. When he died, the trend office died with him. We've lost a lot of ground in terms of fashion credibility since them."

Pam spoke up. "Samantha's helping with that. She's a forward thinker and has done wonders since we acquired her magazine, *Retrofit*. Keep up the good work, Samantha. Is everything on track for the photo shoot?"

"Sort of. Like I said, there's a small hiccup with the factory backdrop but I'm pretty sure I can work it out."

Otto's brows pulled together. "What do you need a factory for? We don't make the clothes, we sell them."

Pam laughed. "That's what makes Samantha's idea so great. She proposed shooting the fully accessorized models against the interior of an empty factory. The juxtaposition will be perfect for the lady-like suit trend of the season."

"If it's an empty factory you need, I can help you out," Otto said. "One of my buddies has a factory. Go back to work and I'll make some calls." He smiled.

"I've seen a lot of factories already," I said. "What's your friend's name?"

"Vito Cantone."

CURTAINS

$\mathcal{I}$f I wasn't screwed before, I was now. No way could I decline Otto's offer. *Be careful what you wish for, Samantha. You just might get it.*

"How do you know Vito?" I asked. My voice rose slightly, but since Otto and Harry had just met me, they probably wouldn't notice. I hoped.

"One of his factories produces our private label bedding," Otto said. "Something else, too," he said, and looked to his brother for help.

"Our curtain collection," Harry added.

"Curtains, that's right." Otto smiled. "I should have an answer for you by the end of the day."

I returned his smile with a feeble one. If this didn't work out, it was going to be curtains for *me.*

After the Tradava brothers and Pam left, I buckled down on work. I propped the concept boards against the wall behind Nancie's empty desk and made a few notes. Begrudgingly, I added *Vito Cantone* to the factory section. I added a question mark and a frowny face next to his name.

At about four, I called Eddie. "Is the visit over?"

"Finally. I can't believe the store manager told me to baby sit some mob wives while the company owners walked the store."

"About that…can you come up here? I need your opinion on something private."

Nothing motivated Eddie like potential insider information. "Be right there." He arrived a few minutes later.

"What, no coffee?" I asked.

"I've bought the last five cups of coffee. You have a paycheck now. I'm boycotting your habit until you reciprocate."

"Fine." I opened a drawer and pulled out a small bag of dark chocolate covered espresso beans. "Go crazy."

He tore the bag open and popped a handful into his mouth. "Whah goih oh?" he asked.

"What's going on is this: last night someone smashed the windows of Nick's showroom. The showroom was sealed because of the murder, but the break-in compromised the evidence. Loncar called Nick and I was at Nick's so I went with him."

"I'm sure that went over well."

"Actually, Nick's still acting weird."

"You mentioned that. Did something else happen?"

"A lot of something else's happened. The weirdest one was that after we left Loncar, we went to Brother's Pizza—"

"What's weird about that? You eat there every other night."

"Shut up and listen to me, okay?" I said. Eddie stuffed another handful of espresso beans into his mouth. "We didn't get a pizza. We got out of the truck and Jimmy, one of the owners, came out and punched Nick."

Eddie choked on one of the espresso beans. He put his fist in front of his mouth and coughed a few times, and then stood up and poured himself a glass of water from the cooler. He threw it down his throat like a shot of kamikaze and then swallowed. After he crumpled the paper cup and tossed it into the trash, he spoke. "Let me get this straight. Nick got into a fist fight last night? How bad was it?"

"He has a black eye."

"Why would Jimmy punch Nick?"

"I have no idea."

"Did you ask him?"

"I tried. Sort of. I was respecting his privacy," I said. Eddie wasn't buying it. "I like my autonomy and sometimes I do things I'd rather Nick not know about. This time the tables were reversed, and I thought it was a good opportunity to establish some boundaries."

"You're the most curious person I know. You're more curious than your cat."

"Leave Logan out of this."

"You know I'm right," he said.

"What do you want me to say? Nick's showroom manager was murdered at his studio, and if that wasn't enough, someone vandalized the place. Anybody else on the planet would have been worried about that but Nick was worried about me being hungry and getting me a pizza. I can help him if I dig around a little, but he hates it when I do that so I'm trying to respect his privacy."

"You're not so good at that."

I sat back and popped an espresso bean into my mouth. I moved it to my cheek like a squirrel and then changed the subject. "Remember how last month when Cat's husband died everybody kept bringing her casseroles?"

"Dude. If something happens to Nick, I'll bring you a casserole."

"That's not it. I went to Angela's house yesterday. After I left Tradava but before I went to Nick's apartment. I wanted to pay my respects."

"You don't know how to make a casserole," he said warily.

"I bought a frozen lasagna at the grocery store. It's the thought that counts, right?"

"I suppose you're right."

"Okay. I thought they'd be in mourning, you know? Somber. But it was like ladies' night in. Angela's sister Connie was there with her friends—two of them were the women who you met today. And an older lady. Connie called her Mama Blum and said she raised Angela. They were drinking Lambrusco and laughing, and they

73

called me 'Nicky's girl,' like Nick was a part of some club of theirs that I know nothing about. They even said that."

Eddie leaned forward with interest. "They said what?"

"Connie said Nick was practically family."

"Do you remember her exact words?"

"Why? That's the gist."

"I might need more than the gist. What did she say?"

"It was vague. She said when Nick hired Angela, he became part of the family."

"Don't you realize what she was saying?"

"That they've taken him under their wing because he was Angela's boss?" The willful ignorance in my voice was obvious even to me.

"You ever heard of the Cosa Nostra?"

"Sure. It's the clothing line of that guy who won *Project Runway* season three."

"The Cosa Nostra is the mafia. The literal translation from Italian means, 'our thing.' It's also known as 'the family.'"

"That had to be coincidence. Right? I mean, you don't think…" I'd been trying as hard as I could to avoid seeing the unavoidable conclusion. "Is it possible that all this time Nick's been connected to the mob?"

WHAT A HEEL

"*If* Nick was a wiseguy, I'd know it. Wouldn't I know it?" I asked. I thought back to the person who'd called Nick's showroom the morning I found Angela's body. *Your boyfriend is not a nice man.* Why would someone say that? "It's not possible that I don't know this."

"He *is* Italian," Eddie said. I glared at him and he grinned. "Joke! Nick's a good guy. I know that, and you know that. Angela's family probably meant exactly what you thought, that they treated him like family because he was her boss."

"Yes, but he acted like he'd never met them. And they acted like he was the son they never had." In terms of disconnect, it was pretty big.

"Loncar told me Angela had ties to the mafia. If she did, then Nick could be in a kind of trouble he doesn't even know about. Angela could have been using his showroom as a front for something." I told Eddie about Angela's personal files having been stolen. "But now that I've got this interview lined up with Carl Collins, I don't know how I'm going to keep tabs on what's going on with Nick."

"Good luck with that." Eddie stood up to leave. He stopped by the door and turned back. "Are you still on track for the photo shoot?"

"I haven't had time to even think about that. Nick's situation comes first."

"You might not be able to do your job and put Nick's situation first," he said. "This situation might force you to make a choice."

"I've known Nick through his business for eleven years—even before we were together. These people aren't that good at hiding their ties, are they? He asked me to marry him. Was I about to marry into the mob? I mean, just yesterday he told me his life was an open book. He wouldn't have said that if he had secrets like this, would he?"

"You wouldn't think so."

"He added me to his car registration and he told me not to knock when I come to his place. He seems to trust me. But I can't help thinking there's something he doesn't want me to know."

"Funny how things work out. Nick finally accepts the thing that makes you go digging around into other people's problems and this time the problem is his." He leaned back. "All I can say is don't drop the ball on that photo shoot."

"Why are you focusing on that?"

"You're officially part of the Tradava fishbowl. They're watching you..." He wiggled his fingers on either side of his head, grinned again, and left.

Great. I finally get noticed for my work and not my extracurricular activities, just when I needed to fly under the radar. If senior management and the store owners found out I was nosing around the mafia, especially during working hours, then I was going to be back out of a job for good. I needed help and I didn't know where to get it.

In past situations like this, I'd sometimes relied on the experience of Dante Lestes, my friend Cat's brother. But Dante's skillz as a private eye were part of a package deal that included innuendo, dangerous situations, and occasional fooling around. Now that I was engaged, I was less in the market for what Dante offered. Cat had told me that Dante didn't believe Nick and I would work out, but I suspected that had more to do with his desire to keep me in a state of unbalance. I hadn't given much thought to Dante since slipping Nick's mother's heirloom ring onto my ring finger, but I knew now that, despite whatever help Dante could provide, he wasn't the right person to ask.

I was going to have to figure out a way to snoop while it looked to the rest of the world like I was going about my life. And there was pretty much one person I could think of who repeatedly badgered me for information. Carl Collins from the *Ribbon Times*.

Before I had a change of mind/heart/attitude/crisis of conscience, I called him.

"Collins," he said.

"Collins, it's Kidd." I paused for a moment. "Samantha Kidd."

"Too bad. I was expecting James Bond. Whatcha got for me?"

"I don't have anything for you right now."

"What about our interview? I'm going through with the whole photo shoot thing so I can get the details on this latest case of yours. Mob ties to a shoe designer. I'm thinking 'What a Heel: Shoe Designer Brings Mob to Ribbon' or 'Scuff Marks: Local Shoe Designer Involved in Dirty Business.'"

"Knock it off, Carl."

"You're right, those titles need work. But it looks to me like your future husband stepped in something and it sure doesn't smell like a rose."

"You talked to Nick?" I asked. "When?"

"This afternoon. He didn't tell you? I went to your house earlier today. Thought you were bailing on me. Found him instead. Good thing, too. I got a nice firsthand account of what happened at his showroom last night."

"He talked to you about the vandalism? On or off the record?"

"Taylor's not an idiot. He knows I'm press, and he knows how it works. Would have been better if *somebody* had called me from the scene, but I'll take what I can get. Who gave him the shiner?"

"Why didn't you ask him?" Carl was quiet. "You *did* ask him, and he didn't tell you. What makes you think I will?"

"It's called investigation. Ask questions, nose around a bit. Sometimes the best information turns up in the unlikeliest place."

It bothered me how on the money Carl was about that. "You said you were in my house?"

"Yeah. Took a peek in your trash can. You really like pretzels."

"That's hardly a scoop." I was about to close down my computer when Nick's email with the pictures of the factories caught my eye. "I'm calling with an update on the interview. I was hoping to have things lined up by now but I'm having some trouble securing a factory setting. We might have to postpone until next week."

"Sorry, Charlie, no dice. My editor approved the interview, the photographer, and the cover story of the Sunday *Style Section*. Said it's been awhile since we did something on fashion, but it's this Friday or not at all."

"That's in two days!" I said.

"I know. You should have thought about that before you pitched me the idea."

To recap: I had a great idea, pitched it to both the local paper and my bosses, got everyone on board, and now had forty-eight hours to make it happen. My employer, duly impressed with my idea, was pulling strings so I could use a factory owned by a businessman of questionable background right about the same time I'd learned that a group of mob wives were throwing a fundraiser for my fiancé.

And on top of everything, I was going to have to stop eating at my favorite pizza joint.

I left the office. Nick was waiting for me in the shoe department, talking to Pam.

"Samantha, I knew we could count on you," Pam said.

I looked back and forth between their faces. "What did I do now?"

She laughed. "Nick said he can get us the shoes for the photo shoot."

"But the interview is in two days and you can't get a sample here by then, can you?"

"You can use the sample from Christmas," he said. "Remember? The forty pair of shoes I gave you?"

"Those were for me," I said. Whoops, that was definitely *not* Samantha 2.0. "But you're right. Perfect solution."

"Outstanding," Pam said. She put her hand on his arm. "Always a pleasure, Nick."

"Pleasure's all mine." They did the air-kiss thing and Pam left.

"The last time we talked, I hadn't formally asked you about the shoes," I said.

"Forget about it."

"Did you say 'Fuhgeddaboudit'?"

"I said forget about it." He gave me a funny smile that suggested he wasn't sure if I was making a joke. "I don't want you to worry. I called in a favor to the factory in Italy. They already have the pattern for the new platform pump and they assured me they have plenty of black suede in inventory. That might be the single style in my collection for fall, so I'm going to need all the exposure I can get." He put his hand on the small of my back and guided me toward the employee exit.

I gave Nick his keys and he drove us to his apartment. My car was where I left it, in the visitor space in the underground parking garage. He parked his truck in his reserved space and we got out.

He walked around the front of the truck, put his finger under my chin, and tipped my face up so we were inches apart and he was staring directly into my eyes. "Would you like to come to the apartment? Get a raincheck on a home cooked meal? I seem to recall Loncar's call last night interrupted us before you had your weekly requirement of meatballs." He leaned down and kissed me. "I fed Logan and cleaned his litterbox before I came to get you. He's set for the night."

"Sure," I said, temporarily distracted from my newfound concerns over Nick's potential mafia ties. He slipped his warm hand into the collar of my jumpsuit and cradled my neck, this time kissing me a little less innocently. I kissed him back until the incongruous backdrop of cars whizzing past us in the parking garage became too hard to ignore.

I pulled away from him. "We should get upstairs."

"My dad's upstairs."

"And half of your neighbors are down here. Either way, I'd prefer a little privacy."

He draped his arm around my shoulder and led me to the elevator. Minutes later, we entered his apartment. The kitchen smelled of melted cheese and garlic.

"Hey, you two," Nick's dad said. We had yet to agree on an appropriate title for me to call him, so for the time being, we were hanging out in "hey" territory.

"Hey," I said.

Nick stifled a smile and shook his head.

"Whoa! Nice shiner. What did you do?"

"It's nothing," Nick said.

Nick Senior looked to me for an explanation.

"I think it was a case of mistaken identity," I said.

"You were there?"

Nick shot me a look that said I was not supposed to tell his dad about his having been assaulted in a parking lot by the owner of a pizza store. It did seem like a possible don't-tell-my-dad story, and it was nice to discover Nick had one of those instead of it always being me.

"I refuse to answer on the grounds it may incriminate me," I said instead.

"I have ways of making you talk," Nick Senior said.

I pantomimed zipping my lips and locking them, and then tossing the key over my shoulder. Nick rolled his eyes. "I suspect you're going to crack the second he leverages the garlic twists against the truth." He left us alone in the kitchen.

"There are garlic twists?" I asked.

"Not for you, there's not," Senior said. He pulled a tray of golden brown bread twists out of the oven and basted them with melted butter. Cloves of garlic had been inserted into the top of each one, and I could see the cloves had softened under the heat. My mouth watered, rendering the imaginary zipper/lock/key barricade useless.

"He did tell you what happened last night, didn't he?" I asked. "At the showroom?"

"Vandals," he said, shaking his head back and forth. "The kid's having a rough time of things. I told him owning the company wasn't going to be easy when he bought me out, but he said he wanted to be full owner."

I picked up a garlic twist from the tray, immediately dropping it from the heat. Nick Senior picked it up with a checkered towel and tossed it back onto the baking tray. "You gotta learn to be less impatient."

"That's one of my character flaws."

He laughed. "There's a difference between impatience and getting stuff done. You get stuff done and I like that."

"Hey," I said. He looked at me over the top of his glasses. "The vandalism at Nick's showroom wasn't regular vandalism. Somebody smashed his window with a concrete block. That's not what high schoolers do."

"He get the shiner at the showroom? Something fall on him?"

"No, that was later. I don't think he wants you to know this, but we went to get a pizza at Brother's and one of the owners came right up to us and punched him."

Nick Senior threw the towel onto the counter. "One of the owners? Mitch or Jimmy?"

"Jimmy."

"You know who he is, right?"

"Sure. He's one of the brothers. He's been serving me pizza since I was in junior high."

"He's Jimmy the Tomato."

"I heard that name before." I rolled my eyes up and tried to place the reference. "Why do you call him that?"

Nick's dad shut the oven and gave me his full attention. "He puts the squeeze on people for the mob." He hesitated a moment before continuing. "He's also Vito Cantone's godson."

15

CLEMENZA'S SPAGHETTI SAUCE AND FRANCIS FORD COPPOLA WINE

"*J*immy the pizza guy is a mobster?" I asked.

"Vito Cantone is a mobster. Jimmy is his godson. Draw your own conclusions."

"I've lived in Ribbon my whole life. Most of my whole life. Most of my adult life. Okay, I've lived here for two years of my adult life. You mean there's a whole criminal activity circuit taking place under my nose and I never even knew it?"

"There are bad guys everywhere. You should know that better than most."

"How do you know Vito?"

"I refuse to answer on the grounds it might incriminate me." He stared at me for a beat. "Go check on my kid while I finish dinner." He turned his back on me and attended to the garlic twists.

I went to the living room to find Nick. He wasn't there. I wandered into the hallway toward his room. The door was shut. I knocked. After a few seconds, he opened it up. He held his phone to his shoulder, the display facing him so I couldn't see the screen. "Is dinner ready?" he asked.

"Not yet."

"I'll be out right after I finish up this call." He eased the door shut while I stood there.

See, now this was a conundrum. I was inches from the door, so to put my ear up against the wood would not have required all that much effort. Chances were, if Nick spoke at a regular decibel, I could pick out a word or two without even moving. But Nick was on the other side of that door, and judging from the silence, he wasn't speaking at a normal decibel, which meant he probably didn't want me to hear his conversation. And there was a good chance that listening in on his private conversation wasn't the type of thing featured in the How To Be A Good Fiancé handbook. It definitely wasn't something Samantha 2.0 would do.

Unless Nick was in trouble and didn't know how to ask for my help. If that was the case, then I needed to do whatever was necessary. The ends justify the means. I'm pretty sure that's in some handbook somewhere.

I leaned forward and put my head against the wood. The door opened. I straightened up too fast and made myself dizzy. Nick slipped his phone into the pocket of his shirt. "You're still here."

"My shoelace was untied." We both looked down at my boots. They had a zipper on the side, no laces. "I thought I was wearing a different pair," I added.

"Sure."

Nick's troubles had been weighing on him and exhaustion lurked behind the black eye and the relatively recent emotional mask. I couldn't lie to him. I couldn't let there be secrets between us.

"We have to talk." I put my hand on his chest and applied enough pressure that he took a step back, into his bedroom, then another. I followed. It was like a super slow motion Tango without music or a rose in either one of our teeth.

I shut the door behind me. Nick put his hands on my waist and bent down to kiss me. I pulled away from him. "When I said talk, I meant talk."

"What's on your mind, Kidd?"

"Nick, I'm freaking out here. Your assistant was murdered under questionable circumstances. The next night, your store front was vandalized and there are no witnesses. That's not rowdy high school kids annoyed about going back to school after holiday break. It takes serious coordination to pull off something like that."

He nodded but didn't say anything.

"And I've got this photo shoot for Tradava, and I looked at a bunch of factories today but the one that's going to work is Vito's, and I know you don't want me to use his but one of the owners of Tradava knows him and said he'd make it happen. And now if I do my job, you're going to think I'm going behind your back, but I'm not. And that's another thing. I like my job and I'm good at it. And right now, I feel like I can't do my job without checking with you first and I don't think I'm cut out to be that kind of wife."

Nick stood up from where he rested against the desk. "Shhhhh," he said. "Wow. You've been carrying around a lot of stuff lately."

"So have you. And you're not talking to me and you of all people should know how I get when somebody keeps information from me." I jerked a thumb over my shoulder toward the door. "That right there? You closing the door on me while you're on the phone? That's like a sign in blinking red lights that says, I NEED YOUR HELP."

"No, that's me not wanting my new fiancé to hear about the surprise I have planned for tomorrow."

"You planned a surprise? In addition to the fundraiser at the fire hall?"

His face fell. "How do you know about that?"

"Connie di Sotto and Katie Caprero came by my office earlier today and told me about it. They asked if I would be able to help out."

"I didn't know they came to see you at Tradava."

"Nick, I'm not trying to nose around in your business, but you can't shut me out—not when you need me. We're supposed to be a team now, right? I'm on your side."

"I want to protect you from this."

"But I was there. I found Angela's body. I'm already involved. Keeping secrets doesn't help me, and it doesn't help you."

"What you're suggesting is a little bit of a double standard. Ever since you moved to Ribbon you've had secrets."

"No, I didn't. Those weren't secrets. Those were situations I accidentally got involved in."

"And didn't tell me about."

"I was trying to protect—" He raised an eyebrow and crossed his arms over his chest. I held both hands up in surrender. "You know what? I'm not going to make excuses for my past behavior. Yes, I kept things from you, and yes, I now see that maybe I should have done things differently. But that was the old Samantha."

"And this is the new Samantha."

"Yes."

"Samantha 2.0," he said, genuinely smiling for the first time in days.

"That's right," I said.

"Okay. Just don't go changing too much. I want to be able to pick you out of a lineup."

"Not funny." I gave him a friendly jab and then led him to the dining room.

Dinner led to movie night. It was Nick Senior's choice since he'd made dinner. He made it halfway through *City Slickers* before falling asleep in his chair. Out of a sense of gratitude (those were some good garlic twists), I maintained my silence through the balance of the movie and left shortly thereafter. For the first time in days, it felt like things were normal.

The next morning, I spent an extra fifteen minutes deciding what to wear. The fundraiser for Nick was after work, and if I wanted to get there early enough to help out, I wouldn't have time to change. After the way the leopard ladies had judged my designer jumpsuit, I wasn't going to take any chances. I made a point of always dressing appropriately, even if my definition was a little outside the norm for the rest of the world. I didn't mind standing out—that was part of what fashion was for—but the idea that I'd somehow missed the boat was insulting.

I settled on an ivory cardigan and pencil skirt, nude fishnets, and ivory pumps. Shades of white were empowering, mostly because ninety percent of the world wore black. I took extra care to blow dry my hair, and then smoothed it with a flat iron. Soft makeup and sheer pink lip tint left me feeling rather pretty. As long as I didn't spill my coffee, I'd be good to go.

My day was a blur of appointments with buyers to collect the samples for the photo shoot. Eddie had taken a much-needed day off, and the advertising offices were otherwise empty. The quiet of the office lent itself to a highly productive day, and I mocked up the layout for the upcoming photo shoot and came up with additional editorial stories for the pre-fall catalog that encompassed handbags, shoes, and the rest of the accessories we carried at Tradava. I even dedicated four pages to the men's business. Somebody had to tell them what not to wear.

I left work at six and drove directly to the fire hall. The parking lot was mostly full. I parked in a row of freshly washed sedans, down a narrow aisle, in a spot next to the chain fence at the edge of the property.

A teenage boy who couldn't have been more than fifteen (and that was being generous) sat in a chair in front of the door. "It'll be five dollars," he said.

"I'm here to help out. Did Nick Taylor give you my name? I'm his fiancé."

"Bully for you. I still need five dollars."

I pulled out my wallet and handed the boy a five. "Does that go toward the fundraiser?" I was impressed. Katie had thought of everything.

"No. It goes to me for sittin' here watching all these cars."

"Says who?"

"Says me."

"You weren't hired to work the fundraiser?"

"Nah, my dad brought the food and I'm stuck here until it's over. I'm making my own fundraiser."

I reached over and pulled the bill from his fingers. "My car's twenty years old. It doesn't need watching."

"Suit yourself," he said with a shrug. He sat down on the stool in front of the building and went back to playing with his phone.

The scent of tomatoes and oregano hit me before I entered the building. Row upon row of six-foot tables had been set up, and happy families sat, laughing, drinking, and eating. Frank Sinatra crooned over the loud speaker. I scanned the interior for a familiar face. Along the back wall, Angela's half-sister and aunts stood behind giant vats of spaghetti and sauce and trays of garlic bread. Each woman was dressed in a version of the same thing: tight black sweater, tight jeans, and an animal-print apron. Debbi's was red, Connie's was pink, and Katie's was green. Debbi pointed at me and then waved me over. Her white chef hat was tilted at an angle on top of her platinum blond hair and she laughed loud enough to temporarily drown out Ol' Blue Eyes.

I approached her. "The place looks fantastic. How did you do this?"

"Honey, we sent the men in this morning to set the place up. Jimmy made the food last night and brought it by earlier today. The kids will clean up when we're done."

"Jimmy? Jimmy from Brother's Pizza?"

"Yeah. Jimmy does all of our fundraisers."

"But does he know this one is for Nick?"

"Doesn't matter. Jimmy's not going to say no to a job we ask him to do."

That wasn't exactly comforting. "What can I do to help?" I said.

"You're practically one of us. Grab a ladle. Nicky's busy with the guests, but I'll tell him you're here." Debbi looked at my white outfit. "You bring an apron?"

"No. I thought this was a party."

"It is a party. With spaghetti." She pulled her red leopard-print apron off from over her head and transferred it over mine. "It's going to be a little big in the chest area, but if you tie it tight, probably nobody will notice." She handed me a ladle. "You're on sauce."

She picked up a giant jug with the word TIPS written on the side and set it on the end of the table, then walked away, leaving me and my carefully chosen ivory party outfit moments away from a tomato-sauce stain.

For the next hour, I kept busy ladling sauce onto plates of pasta.

The crowd was festive. Men who probably shouldn't be dining on plates of spaghetti and giant meatballs gladly threw bills into the tip jar. Katie, Debbi, and Connie weaved up and down the aisles with a tray of cream-filled pastries. Since giving me her apron, Debbi had put on a blue leopard print one. Between the three of them, prints from all major members of the cat family were represented in varying hues. Did they buy these things in bulk?

Connie stopped by twice to check in with me. She didn't mention the sauce splatters on my sweater, but I couldn't help noticing I was the one helper who didn't get a five-minute break.

It was clear from the festive atmosphere that the people in the room weren't strangers to each other. Children ran up and down the aisles freely. A card game had started at a table toward the back of the room, and men in suits shed their blazers and pulled up chairs to join in or watch. I watched Connie maneuver Nick through the tables, introducing him to this person and that. Nick had always been comfortable mingling in social settings.

His relative ease at this one troubled me.

The fundraiser appeared to be a success, which would go a long way toward helping him repair his showroom and offset the potential loss of business. On the other hand, something about the entire event, from the kid outside scamming people out of five dollars apiece to the layer of fifty dollar bills floating on the top of the tip jar seemed dishonest. I couldn't shake my sense that this event was more than it seemed. It wasn't anything obvious, but the sum total of too many things for me to ignore.

I went to the kitchen for a glass of water. A chipped wooden table was filled with uncorked bottles of Sangiovese, and a large olive drab trash can lined with a shiny black bag was overflowing with empty bottles of the same. I picked up one of the bottles. The last time I'd bought wine, this one had been out of my price range. The bottles in the trash can indicated the organizers had already been through several cases.

I set the bottle down and uncapped a green glass bottle of Pellegrino. I drank directly from it and opened the back door for a breath of fresh air. A group of kids were huddled around a pile of cards face down on the sidewalk. A girl, probably about eight, stood next to the boys with a wad of cash in her hand.

"What are you doing?" I asked one of the boys.

"Playing three-card monte."

"Do your parents know you're out here?"

"Who do you think gave us the cards?" He held his hand out. "Lady, you in or you out?"

"I'm out." I went back inside and searched the room for Nick. I finally spotted him, surrounded by men in well-tailored suits, by the dessert station. When he failed to notice my flailing arms across the room, I cut through the crowd and grabbed the lapel of his sport coat. "Excuse me, gentlemen, I need to talk to my fiancé." I stepped away from the group, then grabbed his hand and pulled him out the front door.

"Are you having a good time?" he asked.

"I don't know. How do you think it's going?"

"I think it's a success. The ladies won't tell me how much they made in ticket sales, but judging from the empty cans of tomato paste, they're going through the marinara."

"They won't tell you figures?" I asked.

"No, but they must have raised enough to replace the front window, and that's the priority." He seemed pleased by the turnout.

"You don't see it, do you?"

"See what?"

"Look around you. They're serving Clemenza's spaghetti sauce and Francis Ford Coppola wine."

"So?"

"So wake up and smell the cannoli, Nick. You're in bed with the mob." Nick put his hand over my mouth and I pushed it away. "I don't mean to be rude, but how blind can you be?"

His eyes shifted from side to side and he maneuvered me away from the building. When we rounded the corner to the south-facing exterior, he looked straight into my eyes. "Kidd, I've been in business with the mob for years. I've been hoping you'd never find out."

16

BOY SCOUT TO MADE MAN

"You knew?" I said. I flung his hands off me and put mine palm side up in full defensive mode. I stepped backward. "So, Angela's murder? That wasn't random, was it? All this time you've known what was going on?"

"Kidd, calm down and lower your voice. We can talk about this later."

"No, I'm not going to calm down! All the times you told me I should be careful—stay away from trouble, let the cops handle crime—all the times you got mad when I didn't tell you I was involved in a homicide investigation—you were involved with the mob? Don't you think maybe you should have mentioned that *before* you asked me to marry you?"

"You've got it all wrong—"

I cut him off. "No, I don't think I do. Does Loncar know?" Nick stared at me. "I don't believe this." I shook my head and stormed away from the fire hall.

"Where are you going?" he yelled after me. I ignored him.

Anger, shame, frustration, and adrenaline fueled me. I reached the fence that separated the parking lot from the two-lane road out front. The road curved around to the left and right, making it difficult to see if traffic was heading our way. I pulled my phone out of my skirt pocket and scrolled through my contacts until I reached the police.

"Loncar," the detective answered.

"This is Samantha Kidd. Do you need an informant? Against the mob? Because I just found out I'm on the inside. These people trust me. I'll get whatever information you need but I'm going to need protection." The other end of the phone was quiet. "Hello? Detective, are you there?"

"I'm here."

"Okay, listen. I'm at a fire hall about half a mile from the factory district. The place is swimming with them. You come out here, pretend you're a patron. Park in the lot. Pay at the door and you can see everything for yourself."

"What is it I'm supposed to see?"

"Organized crime! They're all right here at the fire hall and trust me, this thing is organized like nobody's business."

"You heard them planning something?"

"No. I've been stuck behind the marinara pot since I've been here, but they've got to be planning something."

"Ms. Kidd." Funny how he said my name, not like a greeting or a pleasantry, but a burden. "I'm going to need a little more information. Where are you?"

"The fire hall at Bingaman and Sixth."

"Why are you there?"

"Fundraiser for Nick Taylor's window."

"What illegal activity have you witnessed?"

"Nothing yet. Well, there's a boy scamming people out of five dollars to watch their cars, and behind the building a couple of kids are playing three-card monte."

"Kids."

"Well, yes. The adults are inside eating Clemenza's spaghetti."

"Excuse me?"

"You'll see when you get here." I looked behind me to make sure no one was listening. "You *are* coming, aren't you?"

"Is Mr. Taylor there?"

"Yes."

"Let me talk to him."

"I can't. He's inside. He's one of them. I had no idea."

Loncar cursed. "Ms. Kidd, go back inside, do whatever it is you did to get them to trust you in the first place, and wait until I get there."

"Okay, good. Sounds like a plan. Look for me by the cannoli."

"Is that supposed to be code?"

"No, it means I'm tired of serving marinara sauce." I hung up.

As tempted as I was to get in my car and drive away, I couldn't. The kid who'd wanted five dollars to watch my car had had the last laugh by parking me in. Until the lot cleared, I was stuck at the fire hall.

I survived the rest of the spaghetti fundraiser with minimal marinara damage. The stains seemed somehow symbolic. I'd shown up dressed in white, an innocent bystander to something I hadn't wanted to see. And now, the marinara had tainted me, just like the knowledge that Nick had an association with criminals. The thing that kept me motivated to stay was the morbid curiosity of an outsider who accidentally gets a backstage pass to the concert of the year.

The biggest violation came from Nick. I'd trusted him with my life and I'd accepted his promise of a future. But this world didn't hold my future. Whatever I accomplished, I wanted to achieve because I worked hard and proved that I could, not because somebody was presented an offer they couldn't refuse.

No matter how I looked at things, I couldn't figure out when this had happened. How it had happened. And the biggest question: why it had happened. Why Nick had gone from boy scout to made man.

Debbi, Katie, and Connie stood by the kitchen talking. They looked up at me. I forced my face into a smile. Until Loncar arrived, I had to pretend everything was normal. I retied the apron over my outfit and returned to my station. The marinara vat was almost empty, and a guy I hadn't met picked it up and took it away.

"Are you bringing more?" I asked.

"Nah," he said over his shoulder. "Party's winding down. Ran outta wine ten minutes ago. Once we move the cannoli, we're through."

"Where are we moving it?"

"Move it. Give it away. You know, move the goods." He laughed at me and then carried the empty marinara vat into the kitchen.

Without an assigned task or a giant possibly bullet-proof pot to stand behind, I felt vulnerable. Nick, who was standing by the door saying goodbye to people as they left, caught my eye across the room. The discoloration under his eye from Jimmy's assault had faded to pale purple. My heartbeat sped up just standing there, wondering if everything I thought I'd known about him had been a lie.

As the last of the patrons left, he pulled himself away from the exit and joined me. "It's not what you think," he said.

"You don't know what I think."

"After what you said out front, I'd say I have a pretty good idea." He attempted a smile and the corners of his eyes crinkled.

"Don't joke about this."

His expression changed from stern brows and strong jawline to regret. Sadness took over his eyes.

The men assigned to clean-up carried the empty trays to the kitchen and had moved on to breaking down the six-foot tables.

Debbi came out of the kitchen and patted Nick on the cheek. "You did good today," she said. "The family loved you." She handed him a bulging black cotton bag with a drawstring. "Should be enough there to take care of the window and the cement. Maybe a little extra to take out your girl." She smiled at me.

Katie came up behind her. "Samantha, we should go shopping together sometime. Debbi and I can help you pick out some new clothes."

I quickly imagined a store that specialized in animal prints. "I don't like to shop all that much," I lied.

Slowly the parking lot thinned. I stood out front with a take-out container of cannoli resting against my hip. When the last of the cars that had parked me in drove away, I pulled out my keys. Nick swiped them from my gloved hand. "You're not going anywhere," he said. "Not until we talk."

"Can't you understand that I don't want to be a part of this? I want to leave. I want to go home and throw out these stained clothes and pretend this day never happened."

"And then what?"

Reality hit me, and my eyes filled with tears that I'd been holding back all afternoon. "And then I want to start figuring out how to get over you."

Nick tossed my keys to the boy who'd been sitting out front. "Pull her car around, would you? It's the black Honda del Sol."

"You're gonna pay me, right?" asked the boy. "She didn't pay me."

Nick pulled out his wallet. "Here's five dollars. I'll give you another five when you bring the car around."

The boy took the bill and jogged to my car. I looked at the ground, not trusting myself to speak. The engagement ring felt like it was burning a circle around my finger. I spun it around and then eased it off my hand. An engine started. I looked up at Nick. "I can't do this," I said quietly. "The engagement is off."

And then, behind me, there was a loud explosion. I turned just in time to see a cloud of black engulf my twenty-year-old car.

A PINK FOOTBALL

I screamed. Nick shielded me with his arm and pulled me down to the ground. The air grew cloudy and dark. I pushed Nick away and stood up. "The boy!" I cried.

Nick ran toward the car. A second explosion came from the ground in front of my car, rocking it backward. Nick disappeared into the smoke. Seconds later, he emerged. The boy was hunched over next to him, hacking into his fist.

"Get him away from here," Nick said. He pushed the boy toward me. I put my arm around him and guided him through the parking lot, toward the street. A dirty sedan pulled into the lot and stopped next to me. The window rolled down. It was Loncar.

I pointed to where I'd left Nick. "My car blew up. Nick's back there. I'll wait here."

Loncar drove toward the smoke. I coughed a few times to rid my lungs of the inhalant. Light flurries of snow blew around our heads. Flurries were typical this time of year, but no forecast of a storm made me look at them twice. They weren't snowflakes, but pieces of ash that had become airborne.

Sirens sounded, and a fire truck pulled into the lot. Men in thick rubber overalls and wool coats ran a length of hose from their truck and focused their attention on my car.

The boy pulled away from me and stood on the outside of the fence. He threaded his fingers through the metal and climbed up so he could peer over it. "Did you see that?" he asked, eyes wide.

"Yes, I saw it. How come you weren't in the car?"

The boy looked angry. "Hey, lady, just because I tried to scam you out of five dollars doesn't mean you should want me dead."

"That's not what I mean. You started the car. I heard the engine. How come you got out?"

"After you stiffed me, I didn't want to take no chances. I was heading back to ask the other guy for the rest of my money up front. Good thing, too."

"Where are your parents?" I asked suddenly.

"My dad's working. He'll come get me when he's done. I can handle myself until then. I'm not a kid."

"Sure, you're not." I turned my attention back toward the parking lot. It was too late to see much more than the silhouettes of Loncar and Nick and make out a few vehicles here and there. Nick's white truck was parked a few spaces away from where my car had been. The other cars in the lot showed signs of having been there longer than the afternoon.

Soon after the explosion and the arrival of Detective Loncar and the fire truck, police cars entered the lot. I stood with the boy, both of us mesmerized by the activity in front of us. Nick, draped in a blanket, stayed with the cops. I didn't know what the explosion meant. At the moment, I didn't know anything.

Once the fire was under control, it was Loncar, not Nick, who came over to me and the boy. Loncar's attitude was gentler than I was used to.

"Ms. Kidd, I'm going to need your statement, but I'd like to talk to your friend first."

"She ain't my friend," the boy said. "She stiffed me five dollars."

I leaned toward him. "If I hadn't stiffed you five dollars, you would have been inside that car."

"Lady, if you hadn't stiffed me five dollars, I would have been watching your car and it wouldn't have gotten blown up."

I stood back up. "Detective, you're right. You should get his statement."

The boy crossed his arms. "I'm no rat. I didn't see nothing."

Loncar guided the boy a few feet away from me. Through little more than body language, I saw the boy shift from defensive to scared. Loncar wrote something in his notebook and then handed the boy a card. The boy didn't take it at first. I wondered how much of this was an act he'd perfected from watching adults around him treat the police like a nuisance, and then felt myself flush when I realized I'd often treated Loncar the exact same way.

Loncar stood by while the boy pulled out a phone and made a call. When the boy was done, Loncar flagged one of the policemen and called him over. The boy and the policeman headed toward the building. The detective came over to me.

"Okay, Ms. Kidd, you want to tell me what happened?"

"Sure," I said. But instead of answering, I burst into tears.

My lack of transportation and subsequent emotional outburst had led Loncar to chauffer me to the police station. Nick hadn't offered me a ride. I didn't know if he knew I was still there. He'd gone inside the fire hall after handing the boy over to me and I hadn't seen him after that.

Loncar parked his car in a reserved space by the front doors to the precinct. We walked side by side to the entrance. I went inside and stood by the room marked Interrogation.

"Let's go to my office," Loncar said. He led me down a hallway and opened a door on the right.

I'd been to Loncar's office a few times in the past and had always been struck by how devoid of personality it was. Today, the cracked and torn desk chair had been replaced with a brown leather one with lumbar support. A pink football tied with a white ribbon sat on the middle of the desk. Loncar picked it up and set it on a stack of recycled file folders on the shelf behind him.

"A pink football?" I said.

"Girls can play football just as well as boys," Loncar said.

"Your granddaughter is six months old."

"Five," he corrected. "I was going to get her a doll but that seemed like a cliché."

"You're trying to do things differently to show your wife you've changed."

Loncar leaned back in his chair. "You think you know people, but you never really do. Sometimes they surprise you with something unexpected. Could be good or bad. Either way, that's part of the package."

"You're telling me nobody's perfect," I said. "But you're talking about Nick."

"I'm talking about everybody. Take me. I spend my days trying to make this town a better place for the residents, but my wife thinks I'm a bad person because I leave the toilet seat up."

"Leaving a toilet seat up and being involved with the mafia aren't the same thing."

"No, they're not." He picked up a pencil and tapped the end against his desk. Loncar had these little habits: clicking pens, tapping pencils, spinning his wedding ring. They drove me nuts. Come to think of it, they probably drove his wife nuts too. I'd told him to stop it once, and he had, but here we were again. He probably didn't even know he was doing it. I imagined years spent with him while he did his annoying little *tap tap tap* or *click click click*, and how long I would be able to take it before I snapped like his wife.

But Nick didn't have annoying habits, or if he did, I couldn't see them. My attraction had rendered me blind to his flaws, and now that my eyes were open, I could see that he had one flaw that was a doozy.

"How long have you known Mr. Taylor?" Loncar asked.

"Eleven years."

"How'd you meet?"

"Through work. We had a professional relationship." I thought about how I'd acted around Nick and how I'd acted around my other vendors at the time. "A professional relationship with flirting."

Loncar smiled. "Did you think he was perfect?"

"I thought he was close."

"Let me ask you a question. Do you think you're perfect?" His question was so unexpected and, coming from him, borderline sarcastic that I laughed out loud. The resulting sound was a cross between a hiccup and a cough. I slapped my hand over my mouth and apologized for my outburst. He kept staring at me, apparently expecting an actual answer.

"I think we all know I'm not perfect," I said finally.

"Mr. Taylor included?"

"He has a front row view of my imperfections."

"And yet he asked you to spend the rest of your life with him. Why do you think that is?"

I sat up straight and pointed a finger at Loncar. "You're trying to trick me into forgiving him. Why? How come you're not arresting him and telling me to run the other direction? You'd tell your daughter to run the other direction if it was her, wouldn't you? And don't give me any of that 'I've changed' stuff. You wouldn't change that much."

"All I'm saying is if you want to be in a relationship with him, then you need to see him for who he is. Not who you want him to be. If you're not ready to do that, you're both going to be in for disappointment in the future."

"There's not going to be any future. I can't marry someone who's been lying to me ever since we met."

Loncar stood up. "Come with me." He walked out of his office and I followed him. I wasn't sure where we were going or why we were talking about my love life and not the explosion at the fire hall or the mafia contingency in Ribbon or the illegal activities that had probably been planned while I worked the sauce station.

We went farther down the hall. Loncar stopped by the last door on the left. He opened it and led me inside a room that was no bigger than ten feet square.

A small table was pushed up along the back, and a water cooler was wedged into the corner next to a coffee station. But what caught my attention was the wall facing us. It was covered with a blown-up map of the southernmost part of the city of Ribbon. Someone had traced the outline of a series of roads on the map, highlighting a long narrow rectangle that was framed out by Fifth Street on one side and Eleventh Street on the other. Red dot stickers had been affixed to the map, some flat against the shiny plastic surface, others curling at their edges. A cluster of red dots overlapped at an intersection at the bottom. The fire hall had been a few blocks away from that cluster.

"What is this?" I asked.

"It's a map of the known mafia activity in Ribbon."

"How long have you been tracking it?"

"Actively? Last couple of years." He opened a file drawer and pulled out a white tube of paper. He slid a rubber band off and unrolled it. It was the same map, but the dots were yellow and there were about a quarter as many. "This was Ribbon ten years ago."

"The mob's been here for a decade? And you've been actively tracking them for the past couple of years?"

"The dots are yellow because we suspected they were here, but we didn't have proof. Thanks to information we've been getting from people in the community, we now have proof."

Loncar was hinting at something but not spelling it out. My brain was on overload and for once I needed him to give it to me straight. "Detective, please, I don't have the mental strength right now. Whatever you're trying to tell me, I need you to just tell me."

I hadn't heard the door open behind us, so when the voice spoke, I jumped and turned around. I was surprised to see Nick's dad.

"The detective is trying to tell you my son isn't responsible for his business being involved with the mob."

"With all due respect, after what I saw today, I'm not sure I believe you," I said.

"You didn't let me finish," he said. "Nick didn't put the shoe company in jeopardy. I did."

18

BETTER OFF NOT KNOWING

*N*ick Senior remained where he was. I stared at him for a long moment. Loncar broke the spell by moving a plastic chair behind me. I dropped into it. He poured me a cup of water from the cooler and then crossed the room and shook Senior's hand.

"Thanks for coming. I know it's late," Loncar said to him.

Senior nodded. "It's time." Loncar opened the door and turned back. "I think you two should talk." He closed the door behind Senior.

I stood back up. "I don't know what's going on here but I'm not going to be a victim."

"Who says you're a victim? The reason I'm here is because in some ways, you're stronger than the rest of us."

"The rest of who?"

"If I tell you it'll just go to your head." He turned a second plastic chair around and sat facing me. "I'm going to tell you something not many people know." He ticked fingers off on his hand. "My son knows. Detective Loncar knows. And Angela di Sotto knew."

"Angela was murdered," I said. "Maybe I'm better off not knowing."

"Too late," he said. He unbuttoned his jacket and readjusted himself in his chair. "I loved Nick's mother. We had a great marriage, and when she died, I was devastated. I didn't know what to do to fill the hole in my life, so I threw myself into work."

"A lot of people turn to their jobs when they experience loss."

"In time, I accepted her death. There wasn't anybody who could fill her shoes, but I missed having somebody to go to the ball games with me, or to watch a movie. I was spending so much time at the showroom that it was no surprise when one day I noticed my showroom manager was a bright, attractive woman who worked as many hours as I did."

He sat quiet for a moment. As the silence draped itself over the room, I felt the energy shift. This wasn't going to be about accusations and blame. Nick's dad was confiding in me.

"What happened?"

"I asked her out to dinner, and that was the beginning of our relationship. I never expected anything other than companionship. When the company hit a rough patch, I needed money to pay the factories. She said she knew some people who wanted to invest. Maybe I was willfully ignorant, but I didn't see the problem."

"Was she married?"

"No, she wasn't married, but in a way, she was taken. She was Lucky Vincenzo's mistress."

Involuntarily, my mouth formed an "O."

"What happened?" I asked.

"When I found out where the money came from, I got mad. I was a single father who owned a struggling shoe company, but I lived a clean life. It looked to me like all that time she'd been working on Lucky's behalf. I felt like a mark. I broke off our relationship and told her to find another job."

"Did Lucky find out?"

"I don't know. I was trying to figure out a way to pay off the debt when Lucky showed up and told me we were square." His eyes filled with tears, and I sensed that whatever had happened had caused him great pain that he hadn't spoken of before.

I reached over and put my hand on his hand and squeezed.

He looked up at me. "There was one place that money could have come from. Junior" —I knew Junior was Nick— "was about to head off to Parsons School of Design in the fall. But same month Lucky told me we were square, Junior told me he had changed his mind and was taking a semester off to work in the factory. Six months later, he accepted a full scholarship to I-FAD. It took him six years to graduate because he worked on the side, but he eventually got his degree."

"You think Nick paid off your debt with his college fund and never told you."

"I've made mistakes. Lots of them. But my son is a good kid and I won't let you blame him for what I did wrong back then. He had nothing to do with this life. Never has."

"That's not true. Somebody murdered Angela and left her in Nick's showroom. And if that wasn't enough, they destroyed his showroom, and then they threw him a fundraiser. Are you saying they're destroying him to get to you? Is that how they work? Destroy your life and then offer you a helping hand so you're forever in their debt?"

"You catch on pretty quick."

"I don't believe it. Angela was involved in something she didn't want anybody to know. I've been clinging to that. The tiny possibility that her murder didn't have anything to do with Nick, that she was keeping some other secret that brought all this on."

"You're part right," Nick Senior said. "Angela did have a secret, but she wasn't the only one keeping it."

"I don't understand."

"About a year ago, Angela di Sotto showed up on my doorstep and told me she thought I was her father."

19

LEEWAY

*N*ick Senior smiled a little at the memory. "She was a pretty young lady. That dark almost black hair and those brown eyes, she looked so familiar. For a second, I thought I was hallucinating. I remember thinking whatever she was selling, I was going to buy."

"She wasn't there to sell you something, was she?" I asked gently.

"No. She said her mom had kept my identity a secret all those years to protect both of us from Lucky, but after he was killed, she couldn't think of a good reason not to tell me the truth."

"And you believed her? Did you do a DNA test or ask for further proof?"

"I didn't need any proof." He looked down at his hands. "Junior's mother had a hard time during childbirth. After he was born, we agreed not to try again. I had a vasectomy. No way I was Angela's father."

"You didn't tell Angela that, did you?"

"The kid waited twenty years to come see me because she was afraid of what Lucky might do if he found out. She asked if she could visit me once in a while so we could get to know each other."

"This was last year? You were still living in New York, weren't you?"

He nodded. "It was before I fell and broke my hip. Once a week she'd come over after her classes were done and we'd talk. She was a bright girl and she had a future."

"You let her believe something that wasn't true."

"If I told her I wasn't her father, she'd either think Lucky was—a bad guy who'd been responsible for a lot of crime on the streets of New York—or that her mom had slept around. I knew her mother during those years. She was a lady. It took me a long time to come to terms with the fact that she'd gotten caught up in a bad situation. Our time together wasn't about her trying to get a line on something. It was because she was trying to make something of herself. I wish I had seen that at along. I would have done things differently."

"Angela didn't start working for Nick until after that. She didn't just show up with a resume and talk herself into a job, did she?"

"She needed a job and Nick needed a showroom manager. I told him I'd screen candidates for him and I sent her his way. Until recently, her secret was safe with me."

"You didn't tell him the truth?"

"I know I'm not going to live forever. I didn't see any harm in letting Angela believe she found her dad and that he was a good guy who started a shoe company forty years ago. Back when I knew her mother, it was my job to take care of Nick. Now he's grown up and somehow it's his job to take care of me. I didn't want to burden him with another problem."

Secrets kept with the goal of protecting people. I knew about those. I also knew it didn't work to lie to the people we loved in order to protect them. Sooner or later, the secrets come out.

"When Nick's showroom was broken into, the only thing stolen was Angela's personnel file. Depending on what was in there, somebody else either knows the truth or believes your lie."

The story of Angela's background and Nick's dad's decision to let her believe something good about it, stacked up on top of the knowledge that Nick had sacrificed his college tuition in order to get the family shoe company out of debt, left me wondering if I was capable of making the same selfless decisions. Hours ago, when I thought Nick had been keeping mafia ties from me, I'd told him the engagement was off and I never wanted to hear from him again. I didn't know where we stood in the wake of that argument outside the fire hall. And then I remembered my car, the explosion, and why we were sitting in a police station after midnight on a Wednesday.

I've heard people say it's important to reflect on how we got where we are. I wasn't sure if this was one of those times.

I stifled a yawn and considered drinking a cup of coffee from the pot in the corner. Nick Senior followed my gaze. "That coffee's been sitting there since this afternoon. You should be heading home. Let me see if Detective Loncar needs anything else from you."

I smiled and thanked him. After he left the room, I stood up and stared at the map on the wall. All this time, I had no idea there was organized crime in Ribbon. No wonder Loncar was cranky. Fighting crime was exhausting.

Left alone in the room, I yawned again, this time not bothering to hide it. The door opened and Loncar came in. "Get your things. I'll give you a ride to your house."

I shrugged on my coat and followed him to the parking lot. He aimed his remote at the car and I reached for the back door. "You're not under arrest and I'm not your driver. Sit in the front."

I shut the back door and climbed into the passenger side, buckled myself in, and rested my head against the seat. Loncar started the car and we were on our way.

"You okay?" he asked. "You're not normally this quiet."

"I've got a lot on my mind."

He pulled onto the highway. "Want to talk about it?"

I turned my head and looked at him. "How do you know what I talk about isn't related to your investigation? You never want me to talk about your investigations."

"It's late, I'm tired. Your car blew up earlier today and I suspect the reality of the past twenty-four hours won't hit you until you wake up tomorrow morning and question if you dreamt the whole thing. I'm going to give you some leeway."

I looked out the front window, the lines on the side of the highway temporarily lulling me into a near-hypnotic state. After about a mile of silence, I spoke. "I accused Nick of being involved with the mob and he didn't deny it. He told me he was hoping I'd never find out. I got so mad that I told him the engagement was off. And then my car blew up. What if those had been the last words I ever said to him?"

"They weren't."

"But what if?"

"What if is bullshit. You can't live your life on what if." The roads were empty, and we were already at my exit. Loncar pulled onto the ramp and then drove the remaining distance to my house. He either had a good memory, or I'd officially brought the police to my house too many times.

He pulled into my driveway and kept the engine on. "If I quit the force when my wife wanted me to, a lot of bad guys would still be on the streets. If my daughter hadn't seen firsthand what life with a cop is like, she might have married one, and I wouldn't want that life for her. If I hadn't taken that getaway to Tahiti over the holidays, my wife wouldn't have wanted me back." He jutted his chin toward the dashboard. "And if I hadn't plugged your address into my nav system before we left, I wouldn't get to watch you wonder what it means that a homicide detective knows the way to your house." He smiled. "Now get out and go spend time with your cat."

"Thank you for the ride," I said. "And for letting me hear the truth from Nick's dad."

"Good guys. Both of them," Loncar said. "Sure would like to see them come out of this one on top."

"You and me both." I shut the door behind me.

The next morning, I woke to the sound of the alarm on my phone. It was six thirty. A note, written in my handwriting, said, "Get up, make coffee, and call Eddie for a ride into work. Your car did blow up. It was not a dream."

Logan woke too. He stood, stretched, walked the length of the bed, and face-butted me with the top of his head. I kissed him and then pulled him into a kitty snuggle and kept him there as long as he let me. I gave him credit for not wriggling out of my grasp for close to a minute.

I showered and dressed in a blue turtleneck sweater, black wide legged trousers with a blue windowpane pattern, and black pointy toed boots. I added a necklace of interlocking wooden squares, an oversized wood bracelet, dried my hair and secured it away from my face in a low ponytail, and went to the kitchen. Eddie rang the bell while my Pop-Tarts were toasting. I opened the door and he stood there, on the other side of my screen door, holding a newspaper out in front of his face. The headline screamed, "Great Meatballs of Fire: Explosion at Spaghetti Fundraiser Raises More Than Funds."

While I was learning the truth about Angela di Sotto's background and Nick's dad's involvement with the mafia, Carl Collins had been busy.

I snatched the newspaper from Eddie and went back to the kitchen. He followed me and took one of the Pop-Tarts from the plate next to the toaster. I glared at him and he bit the corner off. "Read," he said with a full mouth. "I'll make more."

Last night, a sold-out spaghetti fundraiser at the Canal Street Fire hall ended not with a bang but with a boom when a car parked in the lot out front exploded. The car belonged to Samantha Kidd, fiancé of local shoe designer Nick Taylor.

Taylor's troubles started earlier in the week when his showroom manager, Angela di Sotto, was found dead inside his place of business. Further vandalism prompted the fundraiser, which was organized quickly and quietly. It is not known if the explosion at the fundraiser was specifically aimed at Ms. Kidd in a message to Mr. Taylor or if it was a random act of violence.

I put the paper down. "Did you read this?"

"It's on the front page and it's the lead story on their website. I bet half of Ribbon has read it."

"He all but says someone is after Nick and they're using me to get to him."

Eddie bit off a second chunk of Pop-Tart. "I'm not Carl's biggest fan, but it wasn't much of a stretch to draw that conclusion. Just yesterday we were talking about the possibility that Nick was involved with the mob."

"That was yesterday. Things changed."

"So I read."

The toaster popped up with the second round of Pop-Tarts and I snatched them, and then tossed both onto a nearby plate to let them cool. "I've learned more in the past twenty-four hours than I learned through an entire semester on the history of uniforms. I feel like Neo in *The Matrix* after they plugged him into the computer."

Eddie poured a mug of coffee and sat down at my kitchen table. "Last time we talked, you thought Nick was a member of the family. I mean, I know your conclusion was based on Jimmy the Tomato slugging him in the parking lot of Brothers Pizza, but the evidence still says mafia to me."

"Jimmy the Tomato. How did you know to call him that?"

"That's what everybody calls him. Probably because his name is Jimmy and he makes pizza for a living."

"The boy who was watching the cars in front of the fire hall said his dad dropped off the food and was going to pick him up after he closed the restaurant."

"You're doing that thing you do, where you say stuff that seems to mean something to you but to me sounds like jibberish."

"There was a boy hanging around the fire hall yesterday. He said his dad brought the food and somebody inside said Jimmy from Brothers did all their fundraisers. The kid was scamming people five dollars to watch their cars."

"And you didn't pay him. Way to kill the young entrepreneurial spirit."

"That's not it. His dad is Jimmy the Tomato. He has to be. The boy knew exactly which car was mine. When the fundraiser was over, he took my keys to drive it around, but he got out and left the engine running."

"How come?"

"He said he was afraid I was going to stiff him again and he wanted to be paid up front." I broke my Pop-Tart in half and pointed the slightly burned corner at Eddie. "What if his dad arranged for him to blow up my car?"

FISH AND WILDLIFE

"*Y*ou said he was a just a kid," Eddie said. "Would a kid blow up a car over five dollars?"

"No." I bit my Pop-Tart and chewed. After I swallowed, I continued. "But he might blow it up for a whole lot more."

I filled two travel mugs for Eddie and me, cleaned Logan's litterbox, and left him a bowl filled with tuna and cheese flavored cat food. A couple of months ago the vet had declared Logan overweight and we'd both gone on a diet of sorts. But too many life-is-short moments made it hard to give up my pizza, pretzels, and ice cream diet, so I'd compromised. Logan went back to his favorite brand of cat food and I accepted vegetables into my life. Though there were definitely days when the definition of "vegetable" morphed into "it came out of the ground so it must be healthy." And if it was fried on top of that, well, that was between me and my waistband.

Eddie drove us the short distance to Tradava. We made plans to meet for lunch and went our separate directions. I was eager to throw myself into work.

I sat behind my desk and woke up my computer. For the first time since rounding the corner, I noticed boxes stacked along the wall under a sign I'd pinned there that said *Photo Shoot Samples Here.* I printed out the checklist I'd made of samples needed for the shoot and then spent the next hour and a half organizing what had been dropped off. The problem-solving part of my brain was going to have to operate from the back burner.

Possibly my favorite part of my job was planning the details of an editorial layout in *Retrofit for Tradava.* The magazine's approach back when Nancie first started it had been to look to past decades of fashion and use them as a jumping off point for how we dressed today. So many aspects of day to day life had become underwhelming and personal style was on the verge of being frozen in a mashup of nineties grunge and athleisure. My job was to use the glossy medium of the *Retrofit for Tradava* catalog to elevate it back into something that inspired people to shop.

As I moved the colorful skirt suit samples from their boxes to a portable rack on the side of the room, I knew the era I'd be using as inspiration would be the eighties. Not the neon/lace/fishnet trends that so many people associated with the me-decade, but the tailored suits of Chanel, Oscar de la Renta, Bill Blass, and Geoffrey Beene. It would showcase a return to early feminist professional glamour.

Once the suits were hung on the rack, I took my checklist and went into the store. Tradava's promotional calendar had shifted from post-holiday sales to end-of-season clearance. I headed past racks of sixty-five-percent-off markdowns and tables of last-of-their-kind handbags to the accessories department. Pam Trotter and Otto Tradava were talking to the department manager about a new shipment of scarves that had been delivered that morning.

"Samantha," Pam said. "Are we on track for the photo shoot?"

"Pretty much," I said. "I came down to pull the accessories that we'll be using." I turned to the manager. "Can you give me twelve pair of black opaque tights, size tall? I'm going to need some sunglasses and gloves, too."

"Is that your list?" he asked.

I nodded and handed it to him. "The advertising expense number is on the bottom. You can charge us back at cost for the tights, but I expect to need the sunglasses and gloves on loan. They should be back to you early next week."

"I'll go get the tights. Pick out the glasses you want and I'll unlock them when I get back."

Otto listened with interest. When the manager excused himself and left for his stockroom, Pam smiled. "I told you, Otto, Samantha is one to watch. She's doing great things for us."

"Are your factory problems all ironed out?" Otto asked.

"Yes, thank you. The whole thing came together. Well, except for the shoes."

Pam looked concerned. "I thought Nick said he could have them sent in for us?"

I wasn't willing to air Nick's dirty laundry in front of one of his biggest accounts. "Problem with customs," I said. "Fish and wildlife flagged the shipment for inspection. They might arrive, but I don't want to leave anything up to chance so I'm going to expense shoes from inventory."

"I thought the samples you requested were black suede? Why is fish and wildlife involved?"

Darn it. *Think, Samantha, think.* "The factory used heels that were wrapped in lizard skin instead of leather—they had an overage of skins from a previous order and because of the narrow timetable they went ahead with them. If they do arrive, we can color correct in post-production."

Both executives relaxed noticeably. "Lizard heels will raise the price of the shoes, and with all of this pre-season exposure, might be the perfect thing to give women an excuse to buy yet another pair of black shoes," Pam said. "I know you have experience as a shoe buyer, so this isn't news to you. Use your judgment. This may be the start of a whole new trend."

"An exclusive trend," Otto added.

Sure. Best case scenario, Nick would corner a whole new market. I wondered if he'd see it that way when I told him the news.

KRYPTONITE

*P*am and Otto moved on to the handbag department and I peered into the sunglasses case and narrowed down my choices. A top-of-counter fixture displayed a collection of oversized gold frames with colorful lenses. I thought back to the suit samples in my office, and then amassed a pile of glasses that would coordinate with the colors. I slipped on a pair with blue lenses and felt a tap on my shoulder. I whirled around and faced Eddie.

"If you tell me this," he waved his hands around the glasses on my head, "is considered working, then I'm going straight to my office to apply for a transfer."

"You want Nancie's job?"

"Not if it means somebody else would be responsible for the visual standards of the store. Have you seen what they did in the candy department? Ragu thought it was a good idea to cut the flaps off the shipping containers and stack the boxes next to the register. Who are these people? Were they raised by wolves?"

"Yes, you're right. Making chocolates accessible to the buying public is the universal sign of wolf raising," I said. He made a face. "I'm pulling stock for the photo shoot."

"That's still on?"

"Why wouldn't it be? That's my job, and as the owners of the company now have seen, I'm good at my job."

"I assumed after last night your priorities would have changed."

"To what?"

"To helping Nick get out of this. Did you tell him you're using Vito's factory even though he explicitly asked you not to?"

"No, that didn't come up. Besides I don't think he'd care so much about that now."

Eddie looked dumbfounded. "Why not? You said there's a connection between Vito Cantone and Angela di Sotto. And that Vito has mafia ties. How come you're so willing to rule him out of the suspect pool for what's been happening?"

I grabbed Eddie's arm and pulled him away from the sunglasses counter toward the exit. I forgot that I was wearing the sunglasses and an alarm, triggered by the magnetic security device hanging from the glasses, sounded. Several associates looked at me and I whisked off the glasses and tossed them onto the counter.

"Shhhhhh," I said. "Nick and I—Nick and I might not be destined for happily ever after. I've learned some things, and I've seen some things—"

"You're just going to walk away from him after all this?"

"I think Nick is in trouble and doesn't know how to ask for help. If I go forward with the photo shoot, I can check things out from the inside. There will be plenty of people around, so I'll be safe. Besides, I have a plan."

"You're going to make Vito an offer he can't refuse?"

"I'm going to make these people think I'm one of them. You've heard of dressing the part, right?"

Eddie shook his head at me. "This is not going to turn out well."

"Trust me. I know what's at stake and I'm not going to do anything stupid."

"Famous last words." He tipped his head backward and jutted out his jaw, and then flicked his fingers under his chin like Marlon Brando. "Look what they did to my boy," he said in the worst Godfather impersonation I'd ever heard.

"Nobody talks like that," I said. I turned back to the accessories counter and Eddie went off to deal with the visual travesty in the candy department.

The change of scenery from my office to the store provided a safe zone. I admit that I milked my time, but not for the reasons Eddie implied. While the accessory manager filled out the paperwork to expense and loan out the samples I needed, I wandered through different departments. As soon as I went back to my office, I'd return to the problems that Nick had been having. But wandering the store was like cleansing my palette. Until the scent of tomatoes and cheese caught my attention. Like Toucan Sam, I followed my nose, which led me to the shoe department.

A delivery boy held a stack of flat pizza boxes with a large aluminum tray on top. The clear plastic lid indicated the tray held something green—salad, I assumed. The flat box was a no-brainer. And considering Tradava was in the same strip mall as Brother's Pizza, the provider of the pizza was a no-brainer, too. It took me a moment to realize why the delivery boy looked familiar. He was the boy who'd tried to scam me at the fire hall.

The department was mostly empty, but a sign next to a round marble table announced that a trunk show was taking place. Trunk shows, the practice of designers sending a trunk of their samples ahead of production so customers could reserve their choices before the merchandise shipped, was a time-honored yet increasingly irrelevant practice in fashion. In the past, designers would travel with their collection, hoping customers would respond to the possibility of getting to rub shoulders with them, but social media and the inconvenience of travel had changed things. Now, sales reps were responsible for the in-store presence. In a few cases, the trunks were sent without vendor representation and the store staff executed the event themselves.

Today, the disconnect between the January temperature and the sample collection of cotton sandals in front of me told the story of why the department was so empty. The world of fashion had gradually been shifting to more of a buy-now-wear-now practice, and pre-season trunk shows were having less and less success. The pizza delivery was probably the sales rep's way of acknowledging the interruption to daily business and saying thanks to the staff. Very little bought sales associate loyalty like free food.

Eddie had said something about me helping Nick, and that's exactly what I thought I'd been doing. But there was another way I could help him, not related to the murder investigation. If Tradava agreed to a last-minute trunk show using the sample collection Nick had given me for Christmas, Nick could send those orders to Italy to produce and not have to take a total loss on the season. And if I went straight to Pam with the idea, then the rest of the store would have to fall in line.

I pretended to inspect the samples on the table while the delivery boy collected money and made change for the department manager. When he left, I set down the pink gingham sandal in my hand and hurried after him. He had enough of a lead on me that I didn't think I would catch up to him.

"Hey!" I yelled. "Stop that kid!"

Carmen, a petite but powerful woman from Loss Prevention stepped out from behind the counter and blocked his path. "Hold up," she said. She looked at me. "What'd he do?"

"I didn't do nothin'!" he said. He turned around and looked at me. "Oh, crap. You're bad luck, you know that?"

"Thanks, Carmen," I said. "The kid forgot his tip." I put my hand on his shoulder and turned him around, leading him back into the store. "We need to talk."

He shrugged off my hand. "I don't squeal," he said.

"Interesting. If you didn't know anything, I think you would have said you didn't know anything. But squealing implies that you *do* know something. Let's cut to the chase. I want to know what you know about the bomb that blew up my car yesterday."

He held out his hand. "First, where's my money?"

"What money?"

"You just said I forgot my tip."

"Yeah, sorry. I lied." I crossed my arms. "Do you want to talk to me or do you want me to call the police to take you to the station so you can talk to them there? Because I have their number right here on my phone."

The kid looked like he was fully prepared to outwait me. The scent of pizza floated out of the stockroom and I got angry.

"That pizza you just delivered—that's from Brother's, isn't it?"

He shrugged.

"Is Jimmy your dad?"

"What's it to you?"

I grabbed the front of his coat and pulled it close to me. "Listen, kid. The way I see it, there's a very good chance *you* put the bomb in my car. You were mad because I didn't give you five dollars. How do I know you didn't rig it yourself? Why else would you start the car and then leave it?"

"It's like I told you. I wanted to make sure I got my money."

"You weren't entitled to any money and you know it."

The kid looked past me, a vacant stare that seemed to have no expiration date. Unfortunately for me, whoever had taught this kid how to clam up had done a good job. And on top of that, he seemed to be impervious to the scent of pizza, which, after four days, was turning out to be my Kryptonite.

I heard my name and looked to the side. The manager from accessories approached me with a red plastic bin. "I filled out the paperwork and put everything you wanted in here. I can take it to your office if you want."

I kept my hand on the kid's shoulder so he wouldn't try to leave while I was distracted. "Can you take it to Loss Prevention? I'm going to have everything couriered to Vito's factory at the same time so that'll make it easier to organize when we set up."

"Sure." The manager passed us and went to Loss Prevention, barely acknowledging the kid I held in place with my best Vulcan nerve pinch.

The kid watched him walk away, and then looked back at me. "You know Vito Cantone?" he asked, squinting his eyes as if this was a significant question.

"Yeah, we're good friends. Now are you going to talk, or what?"

"You can't be that good of friends. Vito's the one who blew up your car."

MOBSTER CLOTHES

"*D*id you see him do it?" I asked

"Vito's smarter than that. But he warned me to stay away from your car. Said somethin' bad was gonna happen. He wouldn't know that unless he was the one who done somethin' bad."

The kid took advantage of my temporary confusion to spin out from under my Vulcan grip. He took off down the hall of the employee entrance, pausing by the door to turn around and give me the finger.

Kids today.

I made my way back to my office, my mind swimming in thoughts. Vito? Vito warned the kid to stay away from my car? That *did* make it sound like Vito knew about the bomb, and the only reason I could think of for him to know was if he was responsible for it. He was an obvious suspect because of his rumored mafia affiliations.

Up to now, everything had been directed at Nick. Angela, murdered in his showroom and left in his sample closet. The broken window that shut down his business temporarily. Even the threat on the other end of the phone: *your boyfriend is not a nice man.*

See, that still didn't sit well with me. Vito had made a show of congratulating Nick and me on our engagement. He'd offered me the use of his factory for free as an engagement present. And Nick's decline wasn't personal, it was professional. He hadn't wanted to move production from Italy mid-season. Businessman to business-man, that would have made sense. So again, what would have Vito so charged against Nick that he'd kill his own ex-girlfriend and leave her in Nick's showroom?

The other thing that bothered me was that Angela di Sotto was the victim here, and nobody was mourning her death. When my friend Cat's husband had been killed, she'd been surrounded by people who wanted to pay their respects. It had been an eye-opening moment for me, to see what life is like for someone who opens herself up to the kindness of strangers. It had made me rethink the way I lived. It had been the impetus for buying the frozen lasagna and taking it to Angela's family's house.

And what had I found when I'd arrived? Not a grieving family. The only person to show any anger about what happened had been Mama Blum. What had she said? That Angela was never a part of the family. Did she mean the family, or The Family?

I had to talk to Mama Blum.

The problem there was that I didn't fit in with that crowd. Every time I was around them, I'd been the odd person out. The first time I showed up, I'd hoped to blend but I might as well have landed from outer space. And Mama was old school. She wasn't going to break bread with me because I offered her a frozen lasagna. I was going to have to do better than that.

But first things first. Work. As in, the photo shoot.

The photo shoot was scheduled for Friday and there were enough last minute details to keep me too busy to think about Angela's murder. I arrived back at my office prepared to push all thoughts of Vito and bombs and Nick out of my mind so I could do my job.

It was a good plan. It might have even worked if Nick hadn't been sitting in the chair in front of my desk.

He stood up and smoothed down his tie. "Samantha."

I could count on one hand the times he'd called me by my first name. Well, now that we'd become consenting adults, I'd need both hands, but still.

"Taylor," I said. I set my laptop bag on the floor next to the door and stared at him. There was about five feet of nothing but carpet between us but I felt like I was being held away from him by an invisible barrier. I could smell his cologne, a combination of cedar and sandalwood and something else that now lingered on my sheets at home.

I unbuttoned my coat and hung it on the rack by the door, and then picked up my bag. In order to do my job, I was going to have to go to my desk. And in order to get to my desk, I was going to have to walk right past him. And in order to walk right past him, I was going to have to infiltrate the imaginary barrier and ignore the way his dark hair curled, his brown eyes crinkled, and his masculine scent that rendered me slightly weak.

"I talked to your dad last night," I said.

"I know."

"I didn't know."

"I know."

It was the most unimaginative conversation we could have had after what I'd learned last night. Nick put his hands into the pockets of his coat and looked down for a moment, and then back up at me. "I came here to tell you that I'm not going to have the samples sent from Italy. I know you need them for your shoot, but I thought it would be worse to have them here and then not be able to produce them for your customers."

"I don't understand," I said. "You would have the next four months to produce the order."

"Not if I close the company." His eyes, that he'd kept diverted from mine originally, were now focused on me in a direct stare, their clear, root-beer-barrel shade of brown tinted with hopelessness. "It's better for Tradava if you advertise shoes you'll be able to sell. Otherwise there will be angry customers, and they'll shop elsewhere. That's the worst thing for a retailer."

I wanted to cross the room, take his hand, and convince him there was another way, but the tension between us was too great.

"You can't close the company. It's your dream, your life. I can help you with this."

"If you have another idea, I'm listening. But right now, all I can see is that Angela was murdered and they're after me for a debt I didn't know I carried. I can start a new company when this is over. I might have to take a job designing in-house for another company first. Maybe it won't be shoes. Maybe it'll be leather goods, or handbags, or designer dog leashes. I can consult or look into teaching at I-FAD."

"You can't stop being a shoe designer. It's what you love."

"I wouldn't be the first designer to file for bankruptcy and then reorganize. It happens all the time."

I knew he was right. In my experience at Bentley's New York before moving to Ribbon, I'd seen it several times. Designers who were often the darlings of the media were one step away from bankruptcy court. Fashion was a weird business, one where success wasn't defined by bank statements but by popularity on the pages of magazines and mentions on red carpets.

The acknowledgment of potential professional disaster from Nick was too much. I stepped toward him. He stepped toward me. I held out my hands and he took them in his.

"There has to be something we can do," I said. "These people aren't going to take that away from you."

He bent his head down and rested his forehead against mine. "Too many people are getting hurt," he said quietly. "I won't risk them getting to you." He lifted his head and kissed my forehead, squeezed my hands, and left.

In terms of life problems, this one was big. But inside the very big problem was a tiny ray of light: Nick wasn't a bad guy. He didn't tell me to mind my business, or to let the cops do their thing. He said if I had an idea, he'd listen.

I was going to come up with an idea if it killed me.

After Nick left, I spent the next hour boxing the samples for the photo shoot, and then called Ragu and arranged for delivery to pick them up and courier them to the factory the next day. Fortunately, the store's schedule was light, and the last-minute arrangements were overlooked. It was closing in on six and by the time Eddie came to give me a ride home, I had a plan.

"Do you own anything pinstriped?" I asked.

"I know how your mind works and that question cannot lead anywhere good." Eddie took a swig from a plastic water bottle.

"I've been thinking. I need to talk to someone who knew Angela, and not the women who were here the other day. They think I'm a joke. Do you know they asked me to go shopping with them? Said they could help me with a new look?"

Eddie spit out his water. "I would have paid good money to see the look on your face."

"That's just the thing. I know how to dress. I know how to fit in. Yes, I tend to like clothes that make me stand out but that's because somebody has to inspire the rest of the world to step away from the yoga pants. But it wasn't like that. It was like they look at me and they see a schoolmarm."

"And this leads to my ownership of pinstripe how?"

"Well, I was thinking if I want them to trust me, I need them to see me as one of them. And all things considered, I can't march in there with Nick, and I'd rather not march in there alone."

I told him what I had in mind and we spent the next hour shopping for mobster clothes.

Eddie, who had gotten bored during his lunch break and painted the tips of his peroxide-dyed hair a disturbingly pretty shade of aqua, needed a shower more than I did. He carried his garment bags upstairs and locked the door behind him.

I took advantage of the Nick-less night and ordered a pizza from Brother's. My recent making-friends-with-the-neighbors initiative—part of Samantha 2.0—had me delivering pizzas to the wrong houses so I had a built-in excuse for knocking on said neighbor's doors.

Tonight, I had the pizza delivered to Mrs. Iova across the street. She'd lived there my whole life, but I barely knew her. Judging from how often I saw her watching me from behind the curtains, she'd shown an interest in getting to know me too.

Unlike the neighbors who had already been through this

routine, Mrs. Iova didn't have a stash of petty cash from me to cover such situations. I had about twenty minutes before the pizza was scheduled to arrive and therefore had to change fast.

It took ten minutes to trade my pantsuit for the blue leopard printed skirt suit I'd bought at Tradava. It would have taken less, but the skirt was so tight I needed two pair of Spanx.

After changing, I used half a can of hairspray to volumize my hair and dabbed myself with a sample of Dolce & Gabbana perfume. I added oversized gold hoop earrings and black platform pumps from the sample collection Nick had given me for Christmas. I snipped the tags off a large black and white zebra-printed fake fur stole. The amount of animal print in my outfit would have sent off hostile vibrations in any jungle. I colored my lips in a dark berry shade and slipped on a pair of gold sunglasses with blue frames. The overall effect was a bit frightening in its accuracy.

I slipped an emergency twenty into my padded bra, not because I thought I'd need it, but because hiding money in my unmention-ables felt a bit risky in an I-know-something-you-don't way, and considering I didn't think I knew anything, I couldn't see how this would hurt.

I checked on Logan, gave him a solid fifteen minutes of chase-the-laser exercise, and then peeked out the windows. It felt strangely fulfilling to be the one to spy on Mrs. Iova for once. Unfortunately, I'd timed my peeping Tom routine a little too late and found Mrs. Iova standing on her doorstep with a pizza deliveryman, pointing directly at my house.

What made it worse was that the deliveryman was none other than Jimmy the Tomato himself.

JIMMY THE TOMATO

*J*immy the Tomato didn't deliver the pizzas. Not since I was in high school. And even though I had a file on my computer of ways to get Mrs. Iova back for her nosy neighbor routine, I couldn't let her stand out there with a man who was quite possibly involved in a murder. I ran out of my house, stumbling slightly over the stairs thanks in equal parts to the platform shoes and the blue-tinted sunglasses.

Traffic on my street was usually limited to those who lived on it, and tonight was no different. I crossed the road without incident and quickly reached Mrs. Iova and Jimmy.

Mrs. Iova was in head to toe mauve: mauve cable knit sweater, mauve knit pants that I would bet had an elastic waist. Her auburn hair looked like it had been fresh from the stylist two days ago and she'd been trying to keep the look going. One side of curls appeared slightly flattened. I silently guessed she was a side sleeper.

On the other hand, Jimmy looked like he didn't sleep much and showered even less. I'd always assumed it was because he spent so much time near a pizza oven. Nick's eye was almost faded. Jimmy's was a pale shade of yellowish green, like the lemon-lime flavor of Gatorade.

His eyes swept me from head to toe. "That's a new look for you, isn't it?"

"You know me, I'm always trying new fashions."

He nodded approvingly. "That's a good one. You should keep it up." He held up a dark red insulated bag with one hand and looked at Mr. Iova. "Got your pizza here."

"I think someone must have made a mistake," I said. "I called in an order for a pizza about half an hour ago."

"I know," Jimmy said. "I took the call. You gave this address. Seems we've been getting a lot of requests for delivery to the houses around yours. Always the same order, too. Large round, extra cheese."

"That's hardly a unique pizza," I said.

"Always paid in cash."

"A lot of people pay in cash."

"Extra oregano on the side."

"I read an article about the health benefits of oregano. High antioxidants. You should put that on your menu, tap into the health food market." I looked at Mrs. Iova. "Come to think of it, that was in the *Ribbon Times*. You still have the paper delivered, right? You probably read the same article that I did. Maybe this *is* your pizza."

"I *would* get the *Times* if you'd stop taking it from my lawn whenever your name shows up in it," Mrs. Iova said. "And no, this is not my pizza. I'm lactose intolerant."

Considering she seemed to be offended by both my presence on her porch and my choice of dinner, I was a little surprised she hadn't slammed the door on us and called the police. If Detective Loncar showed up, I didn't think he'd accept that my outfit was purely motivated by the changing tides of fashion.

"Follow me," I said to Jimmy. "I left my wallet inside the house."

I thanked Mrs. Iova (for nothing) and turned toward my house. Across the street, my front door opened, and Eddie came out.

The problem was, Eddie's makeover was more thorough than mine.

He was dressed in a black cashmere topcoat over a double-breasted suit with a pinstripe that was visible from a hundred feet away. Black dress shirt. White necktie. His peroxide-blond hair, now slicked back from his face, appeared darker thanks to a generous application of gel. Aviator glasses hid his eyes.

Mrs. Iova cleared her throat. "Well, I never," she said.

Eddie crossed the street. "You okay out here, babe?" he asked.

Babe? I mouthed. He grinned and draped an arm around my shoulder. "Everything cool?"

"Pizza delivery mix-up," I said.

"It wasn't a mix-up," Mrs. Iova said.

"Tell you what," Jimmy said. "Once you pay me, you can figure out what you want to call this. I gotta get back to the shop."

I turned to Eddie. "*Honey*, do you have your wallet?"

He patted down his pockets. "Must have left it inside the house."

"Fine," I said. I unbuttoned the top two buttons of my blue leopard-printed jacket and reached inside my bra for the twenty. "Keep the change," I said to Jimmy.

"Don't worry. This baby's getting framed and going behind the bar." He put the bill in his pocket and took off.

I handed Eddie the pizza. "I need a minute with my neighbor. Put this in the oven. No time to eat it now."

Eddie carried the pizza across the road and disappeared into my house. I turned to Mrs. Iova to apologize. This hadn't gone exactly as I'd wanted.

"I've been meaning to come over and say hello. We've been neighbors for a few years now, and maybe it's a good idea for us to know each other a little better."

Mrs. Iova crossed her arms over her mauve cable knit sweater. "Samantha, my son went to elementary school with you. I've seen you run around that lawn in your Underoos. There was a time when I thought you were going to grow up into a nice young lady, but that did not happen. The parade of men you have coming and going from your house is enough to make my head spin."

"You have it all wrong. I'm engaged now. I'm going to settle down."

"You're engaged to that hoodlum?" she asked, pointing to my house.

"No, not to him. He's just a friend. I'm engaged to one of the other ones."

"Does your fiancé know you have plans with your *friend* tonight?"

"Well, no, but he doesn't have to know everything I do," I said.

"Hmph. I'm just glad my boy never wanted to date you. Probably would have ruined his life." She stepped inside and slammed the door in my face.

I ran back across the street and slammed my door, this time behind me.

"'Babe?'" I said to Eddie. "And what was with the arm around me? Where did you get that?"

"Last minute substitution. I didn't think 'Dude' was going to cut it. I just sort of channeled Dante. You do know he would have been better at this than me, right?"

"I can't call Dante for help. Not with this, not now, probably not ever. You're going to have to do." I stepped back and assessed him. "You look like an extra from *Robin and the Seven Hoods*."

"You look like an extra from *Married to the Mob*," he countered.

I pulled on a gigantic zebra-printed faux fur collar that slightly resembled the kind of neck brace you get after whiplash and secured it around my neck. "Let's do this."

Eddie drove his VW Bug to Connie di Sotto's house. I instructed him to drive past and circle around the block, and then park along a side street. It was slow going thanks to the unfamiliarity of walking on stiletto-heeled platform pumps, but we made it.

"So, what's the plan?" Eddie asked.

"It's not so much of a plan as a goal. We need to talk to Mama Blum."

"What time does she expect us?"

"She doesn't."

He stopped. "We're just showing up? With nothing?"

"The last time I showed up, I had a frozen lasagna and it wasn't all that appreciated. I'm not going to take a chance on doing something else that makes me look like I'm not one of them. The goal is to get to Mama Blum and find out about Angela. Nobody else is talking about her and I got the distinct sense that Mama is mad about *something* and I want to find out what."

"What's our cover story? Why are we here?"

"To pay our respects to Mama."

"If you're good to Mama, mama's good to you?"

"Something like that."

Eddie turned around and looked in the direction of his VW Bug. "If you get my car blown up, you're going to owe me bigtime."

"Nobody's getting blown up. Come on."

I adjusted the tilt of my sunglasses and rang the doorbell. After a few moments, it opened and we were face to face with Debbi.

"Samantha?" Debbi said. She stood back and looked me up and down. "You look *great.*"

"Hi," I said. "I hope we didn't come at a bad time. I feel like I didn't properly pay my respects to Mama when I was here earlier in the week." The obvious next thing would be for her to invite us in— wasn't it? Or were we supposed to just take the liberty? Maybe I looked the part, but I sure wasn't acting it. I leaned forward and peeked inside. "Mama is here, isn't she?"

"Yes, she's in the salon. I don't think she was expecting any more company, but I guess in your case it doesn't matter. What are you standing there for? You're gonna freeze."

I stepped into the foyer and Eddie followed. Having sacrificed the warmth of a coat for the style of the zebra printed faux fur wrap, I found myself still cold even after the door closed behind me. Eddie unbuttoned his topcoat but kept it on as well. I turned around and saw Debbi eyeing Eddie like a piranha might size up a cow. "I don't know you. You're a friend of Samantha's?"

"Haven't you met?" I said. "This is Eddie the Painter." Eddie glared at me.

"Painter?" Slowly she smiled and ran her hand through her platinum blond hair. Then she pointed at him. "You did that job over on Chestnut Street, didn't you? That was a good one."

Eddie looked uncomfortable, but it might have had something to do with his pointy-toed shoes. "You know I can't talk about that," he said.

She patted his cheek with her open palm. "If I were twenty years younger…"

I think we were all happy she didn't finish that thought.

"They're in the living room," Debbi said. "I was on my way out. Where's your car? You didn't park me in, did you?" She opened the front door again.

"We parked out of the way. You'll be fine."

She pulled on a thick black full-length fur coat and bright pink leather gloves. She gave us a finger wave and then left.

"Great," Eddie said. "Don't stay too long. We have to drive past Chestnut Street when we're done here."

"Why?"

He looked offended. "I need to see what I supposedly painted."

"I don't think she was talking about exteriors." I leaned forward. Mama's voice was audible—she was talking to someone. "Debbi said Mama had company, but I didn't recognize any of the cars out there. I've been here before and you haven't, so I'm thinking you should play it cool and follow my lead. *Capiche*?"

"Just go," he said.

I stood up straight and checked my lipstick in the mirror in the hallway. I looked good. I looked powerful. I looked like one of them. Whoever was visiting with Mama wouldn't think twice of my social visit.

I led Eddie into the room and discovered the one person who could bust me for having an ulterior motive.

Mama's visitor was Nick.

2 4

JEALOUSY

The look on Nick's face was probably a mirror image of mine: shock, confusion, concern, and a little bit of embarrassment. I had the benefit of the oversized blue glasses to hide my expression, but Nick's was full-on evident.

The problem was, I wasn't there to see Nick. I was there for Mama. But if she figured out that this wasn't planned, I was out of luck.

I took a few steps toward Nick and held out my hand. "Hi, honey, sorry I'm late."

He stood and I leaned forward and offered up my cheek for a kiss. A regular kiss might have been more believable, but if he refused, it would have looked far worse. Plus, the lipstick.

I turned to Mama and smiled. "I hope Nicky told you I'd be coming by tonight. With everything that's been going on, I feel like I haven't had a chance to properly pay my respects."

Mama locked eyes with me and held them in an uncomfortably direct stare that lasted long enough to make me fear looking away. I won the stare-off when she looked from me to Nick.

"This one is good. Cares about other people. Still needs to learn a lot of things but has a good heart." She tapped her chest a couple of times and then smiled at me. "Sit. Let's talk."

She looked at Eddie. "Who are you?"

"I'm Samantha's driver," he said. He looked at me. "I trust you're okay getting a ride home with your fiancé?"

I tried giving him the stink eye, but the glasses hid that too. "I'll call you if I need you," I said. "Keep your phone on."

"Sure." Eddie took off and left me alone in the room with Nick and Mama.

I lowered myself onto the plush sofa next to Nick. I couldn't tell from his body language if he was happy or upset that I was there. We'd have to sort through that later.

"Mrs. Blum, I am sorry for your loss," I said.

"Call me Mama," she said. "You're practically family." She leaned back into the cushions and folded her hands in her lap. "My Angela, she didn't deserve what happened. She didn't deserve this life. When her mother died, I tried to protect her, but I could only do so much."

"What happened to Angela's mother?" I asked.

"Angela's mother was killed in a car accident when Angie was four. Angie moved in with me and the girls. Connie accepted her, but Debbi was jealous. Jealousy is a bad emotion. It controls people. Keeps them from taking care of each other. That's why Angie wanted to find out the truth." Mama looked at Nick this time. "Angie was so happy the day she met you. To learn that she had a brother, someone she could look up to, that meant the world to her. At least she had that before she was killed."

"But Nick's dad—" I started to say. Nick put his hand on mine and squeezed it. I studied his face. If he was thinking what I was thinking, then Mama still believed Nick's dad was Angela's father. They all did.

Mama spoke again, this time so quiet I had to lean forward to hear her. "I had two daughters, Debbi, and Angie's mother. Debbi always knew what she wanted. She got into this life by choice and took every piece of it that came her way. Her sister was different. She didn't know about her father's involvement in the family, and when she found out she was pregnant, she cut all ties and disappeared. She started over, built a whole new life for her and her little girl. It's no way to lose your child, and the wedge between us was something I had to live with. In the old country, Angie's mother would have put her real family first. We would have taken care of her. But she was worried about her baby and she thought the way to protect that little girl was to keep her away from us."

"You said Angela's mother died?"

Mama nodded. "It was a shock to all of us when Angie showed up. She never asked for a thing, but she was alone in the world. We were the closest thing to family she had. We opened up our house and let her in, but trust me, that girl never wanted to be a part of our family."

While we were sitting in the living room talking, the front door opened and closed. Debbi's voice rang out. "Mama?" She came into the living room. "You're still here." She looked around. "Where's your other friend? The painter?"

"He heard about a sale at Glidden and had to go."

"You mean he's really a painter? I thought that was code." What could that possibly be code for? "I know a lot of people who could use a guy like him."

"Tradava keeps him pretty busy as is. Eddie's not looking to freelance."

"Too bad."

Mama sat up straight. "We're just finishing up in here. I'll see Nicky and Samantha out."

"Fine," Debbi said. Despite being in her fifties, her body language said one thing: Don't nag me, mom. Debbi left the room. Mama stood and Nick and I followed suit. It seemed the visiting hour was over. I glanced at my watch. It was almost eight. I hadn't eaten since lunch and the Brother's Pizza in my kitchen was calling my name. Except that if I got a ride home from Nick, I'd have to explain it.

Nick pulled his coat from a rack in the hallway, and I wrapped myself as best as I could in the zebra striped stole.

"Mama, thank you for talking to us," I said. "If there's anything

I can do to help you in this time of need, please don't hesitate to ask."

Mama smiled and looked at Nick. "What did I tell ya? This one is a keeper. Lasagna, you can learn. Consideration comes from inside."

I was going to regret that eleven dollars and ninety-nine cents for the rest of my life.

The three of us walked to the door. Mama put her hand on the knob, and then used her other hand to shift Nick and I apart so she could look between us down the hall. Seemingly satisfied, she looked back at our faces. "I'm not stupid. I know why you came here. You want to know if Debbi could have murdered her niece."

Nick was the one to speak. "Do you think she could have? Murdered Angela?"

"The morning Angie died, Debbi claimed she was getting her hair done. But two days later, the salon called to see when she wanted to reschedule her cancelled appointment." Mama pursed her lips and looked back and forth between us. "Debbi's got a mean streak that none of us can explain. You're asking a good question," she said slowly. "And I can't be sure the answer isn't yes."

AN INFORMANT

I left the house in front of Nick. I held onto the black wrought iron banister while I made my way down the concrete steps and into the driveway. It was too dark to see with the glasses on, but I didn't want to blow my cover by pulling them off too soon.

"What are you doing here?" Nick asked.

"I would think it's obvious what I'm doing here."

"Don't tell me this is Samantha 2.0. The old Samantha would have done the exact same thing: put herself in a middle of danger."

I took a step closer to him and put my hands on my hips. "Are you going to lecture me? When I did the exact same thing you did?"

Nick closed the remaining distance between us and put his hands on either side of my face. "No," he whispered. "I'm not going to lecture you." He brushed his lips over mine. "I'm going to thank God you're on my side."

The introduction of danger to Nick's life seemed to have an interesting side effect: it made him frisky. And while I liked knowing his attraction to me existed on many levels, I was starting to worry about how difficult it would be to maintain this level of heat in the future when Angela's murderer was in jail.

Nick's tender kiss turned into something more. His tongue flicked against my lips and I opened my mouth slightly and kissed him back. My fingers got lost in his thick, curly hair while his hands glided down from my face to my shoulders, down my arms, and then to my waist. Moments later, they were on my backside, pulling my hips toward him.

"Let's get out of here," he said in a husky voice.

He pulled out a set of keys and aimed them at shiny black Cadillac in the driveway. The lights blinked. Nick opened the door and climbed inside.

"What are you doing?"

"It's a rental," he said. "I thought it was a good idea to blend. Don't tell me you didn't have the same idea." His eyes moved from my face to my outfit and back to my face.

I climbed in and buckled up. Nick threw the car into drive and backed out into traffic. He reached across the front seat and took my hand in his. He raised it to his lips and kissed the back of it, and then held it while he drove one-handed in a direction I didn't recognize. We weren't headed to his apartment or to my house.

We arrived at Vito's factory a few minutes later. Nick turned off the engine and stared at the building.

"Why did you come here?" I asked.

"If they have their say, this is what I have to look forward to. Give them control of my business or lose it all."

"You can't just sit back and let them control your life. There has to be something else you can do."

He reached across the car and opened the glove box. A small black gun sat inside on top of the owner's manual.

"After your car blew up, you told me you thought I was one of them and that we were over. Even if you were out of my life, I had to find a way to protect you. I didn't know what else to do. Now the way to protect you is to give them what they want."

"Nick, did I ever tell you I did my senior thesis on Bob Mackie?" I asked.

Nick looked at me like he was considering the possibility that my level of denial was so off the charts he might have to have me committed.

I kept my voice level as though we were discussing the chance of snow. "Everybody knows Bob Mackie had a successful career in Hollywood. His name is synonymous with Cher, Carol Burnett, Mitzi Gaynor. A lot of people don't even remember those Mitzi Gaynor specials, but if it wasn't for his costumes, they never would have been as successful as they were."

"Kidd, I don't think you're listening to me."

I closed the glove compartment.

"Bob Mackie wasn't just a costume designer. He was a full-on fashion designer. And there was a time when he borrowed money from questionable sources and it almost cost him his business."

"Questionable sources?"

"The mob. *Vanity Fair* did an article about it. You know how there's a stereotype of mob women in glitzy, bedazzled clothes?" Nick's eyes flickered to my outfit and then back to my face. "You see it in the movies and TV. Think Edie Falco in *The Sopranos*."

"Sure, I know what you mean. The outward display of wealth."

"That's because of him. He couldn't pay back their loan, so he worked off the debt. He dressed the wives, mothers, and mistresses of the men he borrowed money from."

I let my words sink in for a moment, and then pointed to the glove box. "That's one solution, but it's not the only solution. If these people think you owe them something, there's got to be another way to pay them back."

"Like offer free shoes to the wives, mothers, and mistresses of the men who want me to do business with them?"

"Make the women happy and the men won't touch you. That's how Bob Mackie did it."

"That's a bandage. It's not a solution." Nick looked like he heard what I'd said, but that he didn't believe there was a way out other than the one he felt trapped in. He opened the driver's side door.

"Nobody's going to look for us here. Come with me."

Nick climbed out of the Caddy and I slid across the seat and

137

followed him. The building in front of us had been vacant for a long time. Light from the moon and the streetlamp by the road cast weird shadows the gravel. The entrance was dark. I reached my hand out for Nick's and held tight. My skinny stiletto heel caught between some broken concrete and my ankle twisted. I stumbled, and Nick pulled me up.

"Are you okay?" he asked.

"My shoe got caught." I said. I bent my foot at an awkward angle and pulled it out of the shoe. Nick freed the shoe from the gravel where it had been caught. The small black heel tap remained wedged between the rocks. If I put the shoe back on, I'd be walking on the exposed nail. Walking on it in that condition would destroy the leather on the heel quickly. Even worse, the nail would provide no traction against the exposed concrete floors inside.

I shivered from the cool air. Despite the oversized fur collar and cuffs on my suit, tendrils of cold snaked under the fabric and left me covered in goosebumps. Making out with Nick in front of Mama's house had temporarily warmed me up, as had the heated seats in the Caddy.

Nick dangled my shoe over his index finger and looked at me. "Let's be dangerous, Kidd. Let's take control. All this stuff around us is making me feel helpless. Angela's murder, the vandalism, Jimmy punching me, and your car. I'm tired of having things happen to me. I want to make something happen. I want to get back at these people."

He pulled his arm back and threw my shoe at the dirty window. The glass shattered and landed inside the building. Nick looked at me. "My whole life was shattered, just like that window. They took it all."

"But why? Why is this happening now?"

"They found out there was an informant and they traced it back to me. I paid my dad's debt off a long time ago. I didn't suspect anything when Angela asked for a job. When she told me she was my half-sister, I acted surprised. I talked to my dad and he told me the truth. That he'd been letting her believe what she wanted to believe. It seemed innocent enough, but I knew what they did to him back then and I wasn't going to take any chances, so I told Loncar."

"Were you going to tell me? It's a big secret to keep from the person you plan to marry. Did you think about that?"

Nick shifted his attention from the window to me. Moonlight cast a faint glow over his face. He looked weathered. "I wanted to tell you a hundred times. But after you saved my dad last year on your birthday, and then the thing over Christmas, I saw how you fight to make things right and I was so scared that I'd lose you. They want me to feel like I have nothing left." He came closer again and slid his hand around the back of my neck. "They don't realize that if I have you, I have everything."

I turned away from him and stared at the broken window. My shoe was on the other side, laying on its side, highlighted by a beam of light from behind us. "Is this how it starts? These people want to get you. They want you to become part of their organization. This isn't you—breaking into abandoned buildings and making out in public places. You aren't the kind of guy who throws a shoe."

"I'm sorry about your shoe," he said. "I'm sorry about so many things."

"Nick, they tried to get your company once, back when your dad borrowed money from them. Is history going to repeat itself? Is that what we have to expect from our future? That one day temptation will be too much and you'll slip up and start doing things their way?"

"No, Shhhhh, no," he said. He wrapped both arms around me and held me close. I tipped my head and laid it on his chest. "Listen to me, Kidd. I'm not my father and you're not a mafia princess." He relaxed his arms and pulled back, scanning my suit. "Although tonight it's a little harder to tell that just from looking." I smiled. He hugged me again. "This whole situation is making me crazy. I don't want you to see that side of me."

"You can't hide your emotions from me. Not when things get difficult. I'm terrified of the future, about how our lives are going to change, about what you expect of me as a wife, and whether or not you want me to give up my career. But if you shut me out, then that's worse. I need to know you have fears too."

He traced his finger down the length of my nose. "I have all kinds of fears, but not about us. I don't want you to give up who you are for me. I don't want you to give up anything for me."

I looked through the broken glass. "I had to give up my shoe. And that shoe looked good with my outfit."

"How about we get your shoe and go back to my place and see how it looks *without* your outfit?"

"Nick!"

He bent down and nuzzled the side of my neck. "It's the leopard print. You should wear it more often." He stood up straight and pressed his finger against my lips. "Save my space. I'll be right back."

He pulled on his glove and reached inside the broken glass to unlock the door. It swung open and Nick stepped inside. He bent down and picked up my shoe, tapped the toe of it on the ground a few times to free it of any remaining shards of glass, and stood up.

Lights illuminated his face and his eyes widened. Behind me, the sound of tires on gravel announced a newcomer to our party. I turned around in time to see a shiny black town car pull into the factory lot and park alongside of Nick's Cadillac.

Vito Cantone got out of the car. "You're on private property," he said. "I got a call that there was a break-in."

"My photo shoot is tomorrow," I said. "I made arrangements for the delivery department of Tradava to bring the samples out and I wanted to see if it had already been done."

"You don't have to lie," Vito said. "I know the real reason you're here."

If there was a real reason to be there, then Nick had kept that to himself. Where was Nick, anyway? Seconds ago, he'd been directly on the other side of the wall. If Vito didn't see him, then he'd gone somewhere. I didn't believe for a second Nick would leave me in danger, but where was he?

"I'm not alone," I said.

"I know. Mr. Taylor looks at you the way I looked at *mi bambina* a long time ago, and I don't blame him. He has the luxury of showing the world how he feels. I didn't have that."

"Why not? Is your world so filled with lying and backstabbing and violence that you isolated your family from it?"

"In a way, yes." He looked to the side of the building.

Nick came out from the shadows and walked between Vito and me. "I won't let you hurt her," he said. "Not like you hurt Angela. She was your mistress until you tired of her."

"You have it all wrong," Vito said. He paused and seemed to consider what he was about to say. ""I could never have hurt Angela. She was my daughter."

STABILITY

"*Y*our *daughter?*" Nick asked, surprised.

"*Your* daughter?" I asked at the same time. The words were the same, but the questions were different. Nick and I exchanged looks. "You're Angela's father?" I asked.

Vito held both of his arms out, open wide, palms facing up. "Please. The police are on their way. My factory is wired with a silent alarm that sounds at my house and at their station. Your friend Detective Loncar will be here shortly. It's been a secret for too long and it's time for me to tell the truth. Let's go inside where we can talk."

It was an odd group that ended up sitting on folding chairs inside Vito's empty factory. Loncar showed up a few minutes after Vito had. If he was surprised by our presence, he kept it to himself.

We appeared not to be the first group of people who met inside the factory for reasons other than a walk-through. A table was set up in the corner, surrounded by chairs. I wondered briefly if the business conducted at this table had included a plan to vandalize Nick's showroom or blow up my car, or if it was just the location of Vito's weekly poker game. My imagination was running in directions I didn't want to acknowledge, and the stones it flipped left dangerous theories exposed in its wake.

"Allow me to cut to the chase. Angela di Sotto was my daughter. I used to think two people knew that to be a truth: me and Angela. I don't believe that anymore," Vito said.

"Why did you keep it a secret?" I asked. Loncar looked at me. Nick kept watching Vito. "She might not be dead if people knew she was your daughter," I added.

"I thought I was protecting her," Vito said. "Understand, I didn't know. For a long time. Her mother and I had an understanding. I gave her as much as I could, considering the circumstances."

"Her mother was Lucky Vincenzo's mistress," Nick said.

"Lucky and I had certain things in common," Vito said.

Nick slammed his closed fist down on the table. "When Lucky died, Angela's mom could have gotten them both out of this life. You took advantage of her," Nick said angrily. "Angela's mother was a working girl who fell in love with my dad after my mother died. She made him happy. But you guys made her feel like property. My dad got caught in the middle of that. The money Lucky infused into my dad's company—now *my* company—it tore them apart. She left him saddled with debt to you. I thought those debts were cleared a long time ago, but you won't let me go."

Loncar spoke. "Mr. Taylor, you best let Mr. Cantone speak."

Nick balled his fists up in anger. "There's nothing he can say to change what happened."

"Mr. Taylor," Vito said, "Angela told me you gave her a job. She told me she led your family to believe you and she were related. That was wrong of her, but I understood why she did it. Her mother was trapped in a life she didn't want, and when she left New York, pregnant and alone, she did that so her baby would never have to feel like she belonged to someone else. Angela was guilty of using you and your dad for one purpose: stability. If she could have chosen which of the two of us was her real father, I have no doubt she would have chosen your father. I can't say I blame her."

Sitting in the dark corner of the factory illuminated by the light from a pool of cell phones in the center of the table, I found it difficult to concentrate on Vito's story. From the very first time Nick and I had ended up here at this factory site, Vito had come across as a bad guy. Even Detective Loncar had known about his criminal past, and here we were, sitting around a card table like we were old friends.

"Why did you tell me to use your factory?" I suddenly asked. "You said you wouldn't charge me, even after I told you Tradava would pay. You said I—we—should consider it an engagement present. What could you gain from that?"

"Absolutely nothing," Vito said.

"But then why?"

"My Angela didn't want anybody to know I was her father, and after all these years, after having built up a network of loyalties"— he glanced at Loncar— "and a profitable business, to find out my daughter was embarrassed by me opened my eyes. I'm not a young man, Ms. Kidd. I'm not immortal or invincible. When my time comes, I will have to face the life I lived. But I come from a life where we find ways to thank people for helping us. When Angela told me Nick had proposed to you, I wanted to find a way to do something for the two of you."

"Angela told you?" I asked. "You said you didn't know. I thought we told you the morning we were here."

Vito smiled. "In my business, it pays to have a poker face. Nick, you gave my girl a job, not because someone twisted your arm or made you think you couldn't say no. You knew she wasn't related to you. But you looked at what she'd accomplished in her life and you made a decision based on that. You gave the girl a life outside of this world, not because you were afraid of me or what I stood for. I thank you for that."

"Vito, with all due respect," I said, "why are you cooperating with the police?"

Loncar and Nick's heads whipped toward me so fast I was afraid their eyeballs would fly out.

Vito's face twisted into anger. "Somebody killed my daughter. If this is about me, then I have a leak in my organization. If it's not, then I have lost my child for a reason I can't begin to comprehend.

Angela didn't condone my life. She didn't want to be a part of it. I told Detective Loncar that I would cooperate with him in this matter so the killer could be brought to justice, because that's what Angela would have wanted." He stood up and rebuttoned his camel hair top coat. "But we're wasting valuable time. If you don't find who did this in the next day, I will take steps toward justice." He stormed out of the factory.

The three of us remained silent until the car engine started and the sound of tires on gravel carried away from us. I looked back and forth between Loncar and Nick's faces.

"What? We were all thinking it," I said.

Loncar turned to Nick. "Everything Mr. Cantone told you here is true. He has been nothing but cooperative with the department since Ms. Kidd discovered Ms. di Sotto's body at your showroom. Mr. Cantone would like you to think he's the victim. Let me assure you, Vito Cantone is not a good man. The victim here is Angela di Sotto. Mr. Taylor, you've also been a victim. But unless I find something to tie Mr. Cantone to the crimes connected to this case, he will walk away from this."

"Why are we here?" I asked. "I mean, I know Nick brought me here, but you and Vito? What's that about? You never let me sit in on your investigations."

"When Mr. Taylor broke into the factory, a silent alarm was tripped at Mr. Cantone's house. There's a separate alarm that rings in my office. I didn't expect to find you two," he paused, and looked directly at me, "though I'm not entirely surprised." He turned to Nick and continued. "I thought you deserved some answers."

"You think those were answers?" Nick said. "That was a snow job. Who killed Angela? Who threw a concrete block through my showroom window?"

"Why did Jimmy the Tomato punch Nick?" I added.

"I can't answer those questions," Loncar said.

"Can't or won't?" Nick asked. Loncar remained silent.

Nick's tone changed. "What do you want me to do?" he asked quietly.

"I can't tell you to shut your doors. I can't tell you to take a loss or file bankruptcy. We released your showroom. What you do next is up to you."

"What about me?" I asked. "My car? Somebody tried to blow me up."

"What you thought was an explosion turned out to be a smoke bomb."

"A smoke bomb? It was just a joke? My car wasn't destroyed?"

"The bomb didn't ruin it, but there's considerable water damage from the hose. We found the device under the front end of your car. It could have been put there by anybody but we have reason to suspect that it was a juvenile prank that went wrong."

"You mean Jimmy the Tomato's kid? The one who tried to scam me?" Loncar raised his eyebrows. "I don't care if it does show the entrepreneurial spirit. I work hard for my money and I'm not about to hand it over to a scammer."

Loncar turned back to Nick. "Other than Ms. Kidd's car, what we're seeing here is classic mafia behavior. Whoever is behind this is connected, and at a very high level. There's a short list of suspects who fit that profile."

27

JUGGLING WET CATS

"*I*'m supposed to be back here in the morning to do a major photo shoot for Tradava," I said. "It wasn't my idea to shoot it here. I mean, at first it was, but when I learned about Vito and all this, I tried to go a different direction. The owner of the store set it up and as we all know, my employment history since returning to Ribbon has been tenuous. How do I know it'll be safe?"

Loncar didn't seem pleased, but he also didn't seem surprised. "I got a tip about that from Carl Collins. He thought maybe you'd forget to mention it to me. I'm sending a team of my men out here to pose as security."

"If Carl called you about the photo shoot, then he's just trying to make it into something more than it is. Did you see the smear job he did on Nick in today's paper?"

Nick put his hand on top of mine. "Kidd, this photo shoot for Tradava and the interview with you—those are both very good things. You deserve to be in the limelight and to get credit. Loncar isn't going to let anything happen, and if Vito is behind this, he's not going to risk damage to his property to get you."

I shivered and wrapped the zebra printed fur around me tighter. The exposed concrete walls shielded us from the wind, but they provided little in the way of warmth. I was tired and hungry. And now that I'd made such a big deal over the photo shoot, the reality of the very big day in my future loomed large.

The three of us left the factory and Nick drove me home. He pulled into the driveway but didn't turn off the engine.

"Tomorrow—your interview. I want you to knock them dead, okay? Don't worry about me or about any of this. You had a great idea and it's going to lead to lots of success for you."

"Do you want to be there?"

"No." He turned toward me. "I can't get Vito's words out of my head. Nobody knew Angela was his daughter. Killing her had nothing to do with him, at least that's how it looks now. I can't put you in danger by spending any more time with you. Not until this is over. I don't know what they want, but it's about me, not you."

Nick waited in the driveway while I went into my house. As hungry as I was, I was even more tired, and the incredibly high amount of Aqua-Net in my mafia hairdo drove me to the shower first and then to bed. Logan was waiting for me on top of the covers.

It was cold pizza for breakfast. Since today was not just about the photo shoot but also my interview for the *Ribbon Times*, I thought it best to avoid any potential tomato stains on my carefully selected outfit. When I finished eating and drinking (cold pizza goes nicely with cold coffee), I showered again, carefully applied a full face of makeup intended to make it look like I wasn't wearing any at all, blow dried my hair into a style about a third the size of last night's, and slipped on my outfit: a light blue pantsuit, navy blue silk blouse, black belt and mary jane pumps. The blouse had an attached scarf-like collar that, when knotted, framed out my neck and face. I transferred the contents of my handbag to a black laptop bag, slid my checklist and notes into an empty pocket, and left.

And remembered that I didn't have a car. Crap!

I called Tradava to see if Ragu could swing by and get me on his way to the factory, only to learn that the samples had been dropped off hours earlier. There was one other person I knew would be at the photo shoot so I called him.

"Carl, this is Samantha Kidd. I need a ride to the factory."

"That's right! I heard your car was blown up. I don't want the story now—not until the tape is rolling."

"There is no tape, Carl."

"I know. I hate it. My entire vocabulary of reporter's terms is obsolete thanks to technology. Next thing you know we'll have flying cars and transporter devices."

"May I remind you why I called? I don't have a car, and my transporter device is on the fritz. I need a ride."

"Be there in twenty minutes."

While I was waiting, I helped myself to another (two) slice(s) of pizza. (I needed all the antioxidants I could get.) Carl pulled into my driveway and beeped his horn. I bent down and kissed Logan between his ears. "Funny how things work out, isn't it? I'm leaving here a regular working girl and I'm coming home the subject of a profile in the newspaper."

Logan, impressed with all that I'd accomplished, meowed and then buried his head in his water bowl. I grabbed my bag and left.

Carl wore a shirt and tie under a brown zip-front bomber jacket. It was like Indiana Jones meets David Brent. On his head was a brown tweed cap that I happened to know Tradava had marked down to $12.99. I'd never seen Carl without a hat. Either it was a stylistic quirk or he had a hairline situation he was trying to keep under wraps.

When I opened the door, Carl moved an empty take-out bag to the back and brushed his hand over the passenger seat a few times to rid it of errant French fries.

"When's the last time you cleaned this thing?" I asked.

He held his finger up to his lips. "No talking. Got it? I am not risking this interview by your small talk in my car."

I sat down and looked out the window. Who knows? The silence might be nice.

We arrived at Vito's factory in about half an hour. It was still pretty early in the day, and even during rush hour, traffic in Ribbon in January wasn't particularly heavy. More people were driving out of the city toward Philadelphia, Harrisburg, or Allentown than the direction we headed. The Tradava delivery truck was parked by the front entrance, and a couple of men I recognized from the store were unloading the boxes I'd packed in my office. Security officers stood by the fence that blocked the factory from the road out front. Loncar had delivered on his promise.

The way I'd laid out the day, we would do the interview first with the factory backdrop. Trying to wrangle models, makeup artists, lighting assistants, and everything else on the same day as the *Ribbon Times* interview would have been a little like juggling wet cats, especially since I'd become a one-woman production.

For the purposes of being interviewed while representing Tradava, we'd all agreed that today's photo shoot should include pictures of me assembling the outfits that would ultimately be used in the magalog, but strictly as samples and not styled on models. This eliminated the need to book additional models, makeup artists, and lighting experts for two separate shoots (The *Ribbon Times* photo crew consisted of a man with a camera. Good thing I'd applied my makeup.) I suspected Carl was going to leverage my relationship with Nick to sensationalize the article, so to be on the safe side, I'd asked the store's PR department to give me guidelines on what could and couldn't be asked. I pulled out a sheath of papers and handed them to Carl.

"Here are the releases," I said. "I'd rather keep things focused on the store and not on the criminal investigations in my past."

"That's not the deal, Kidd. This is a feature on you. A person of interest in Ribbon, Pennsylvania."

"You're not going to call it that, are you?"

He smiled. "I might. In a way, you are Ribbon's most interesting person."

I grabbed his arm and pulled him away from his photographer. "This might be about me but it's also about my job. If you back me into a corner, I'll clam up. That's not going to do anybody any good."

"What are you so worried about? Don't you trust me?" He grinned and adjusted his hat. "Relax. It's just you and me and my camera guy. I'll do the interview first, and then he'll get shots of you with your merchandise."

I pointed at him. "If you so much as mention the murder at Nick's showroom, I'm out of here."

"Kidd, what did I tell ya? That's cabbage. I'd much rather talk about why you suggested we use Vito Cantone's factory as your setting."

"You wouldn't dare," I said.

"It's called background research, Kidd. I know you're raring to give me a quote." He held his recorder out toward me. "From this point on, anything you say is on the record."

I closed my mouth and bit my lip to keep from talking. Behind Carl, a dark blue sedan pulled into the lot. It parked next to the Tradava van and Pam Trotter and the owners of Tradava got out.

"Oh, look!" Carl said. "Tradava executives. Those are the people you were hoping not to embarrass, right?" His grin got wider. "Don't worry, I'll make sure you have a chance to say the store name between stories about all of your run-ins with the police."

28

A PEACH

"Don't even think about making me look bad in front of the store owners," I threatened. I left Carl and crossed the parking lot to greet Pam, Otto, and Harry. "This is a surprise!" I said to them. Once again, nerves caused my voice to rise and crack like Peter Brady going through puberty.

"Are you kidding?" Pam said. "This is the most exciting thing anyone from Tradava has done in a long time. Otto and Harry are supposed to visit the West Ribbon store this afternoon, but I convinced them to come here first. Will Nick be joining us?"

"No, he's busy getting his showroom back together."

"I heard about the vandalism. Is the inventory salvageable?" Harry asked.

"I think that's what he's hoping to figure out today. The police released the crime scene last night so today is about assessing the damage."

"Poor thing," Pam said. She leaned closer to me so the store owners couldn't hear her. "The West Ribbon store has an opening for a general manager. I've got some tough competition, but your idea made me look very good. Make me proud, Samantha." She stood back up. "Otto? Harry? Why don't we find a nice, out of the way spot where we can listen in on the interview without bothering anybody?" She winked at me.

"Vaseline on the teeth," Harry said to me. "Keeps you smiling during the whole interview. Learned about that trick when I married a cheerleader."

"Thanks for the tip," I said.

The Tradava executives went inside the factory. I scanned the parking lot. Security officers stood by the entrance and close to the building. I recognized two of them from the night Nick's showroom had been vandalized. My stress level dropped slightly, until it occurred to me that Carl would be asking about my involvement with the police, and Loncar wasn't going to like that one bit. My stress level rose, and my left eye started to twitch.

Me and my bright ideas.

I trailed behind Otto and found Carl hovering above one of two chairs that faced each other. A table sat next to us. It wasn't dissimilar to the setup in Loncar's interrogation room, a fact I knew from experience. It was exactly the type of detail Carl would want me to share. I kept my thoughts to myself.

"Here's how we're doing this. My recorder will sit on the table and pick up our conversation. You'll also wear a mic just in case there's loud ambient noise. I'll transcribe the interview tonight and submit the story to the weekend editor."

"This weekend? Won't you need time to Photoshop the pictures and fact check?"

"The tie-in with your boyfriend made the whole thing a little more newsworthy than I originally expected. Truthfully, this started out as a puff piece. Remind me to take you out for a drink sometime to say thanks for being in the middle of another investigation. One involving the mob, too. You're a peach, Kidd."

"Yeah, I did it for you. And let me help you out with your fact checking. Nick Taylor is my fiancé, not my boyfriend."

"Wow. Ribbon's most eligible shoe designer made it official, huh? Hope he knows what he's in for. You must be a handful."

"Is your recorder on yet?"

"No."

"Good. Bite me."

Carl rolled his eyes. Behind him, Otto waved his hands back and forth to get my attention. He pointed to his phone and then held his hands palm-side up in a question.

"You can come over," I called out. "We haven't started yet."

He walked up to us. "My brother and Pam just brought up an important question. Has anyone from Tradava reviewed your questions?"

"Excuse me?" Carl asked.

"Standard press procedure," Otto said. "If this was just an interview of Ms. Kidd as a local celebrity, we'd request that she not mention the store. Since we're using our merchandise in the shoot and tying it into our advertising campaign, there's no way to keep Tradava out of it."

I looked at Carl. "It *is* standard procedure," I said. "The store where I worked in New York was the same. Even today I usually just say 'luxury store in New York' instead of Bentley's New York. I'm trained."

Carl looked annoyed. He handed a small stack of index cards to Otto. "Don't take too long," he said. "We need to get this thing started if we're going to get pictures too."

Otto held up a hand and then flipped rapidly through the cards. He dropped the fourth, fifth, and thirteen through fifteen on the desk, and then handed the stack back to Carl. He looked at me. "Samantha, you must have a very interesting background." He picked up the cards from the table and stuck them in his pocket.

Carl flipped through the remaining cards. "He took all the good ones!" he said. "What's he going to do to me if I ask them anyway? I'm a journalist. He can't stop me, can he?"

"He can do whatever he wants where Tradava is concerned. He owns the company."

He turned on his recording device and looked straight at me. "Fashion industry professional. Small town girl moves to the big city and then moves back home. The prodigal daughter? Or a restless spirit looking for her place in the world? Today *Ribbon Times* reporter Carl Collins talks to Samantha Kidd about who she is, what she's done, and where she sees herself in the future. Samantha, before we get into your decision to move back to the town where you grew up, I have to ask: is life in Ribbon as exciting as New York?"

And we were off.

The formal interview lasted close to an hour. Despite Carl's repeated attempts to expose the dark side of my life, I mostly kept things on track. I knew he'd take creative license when it came to background information; every single thing I'd been involved with since moving back home had been covered in the *Ribbon Times* and it was merely a matter of him rooting through the archives.

He finished on a lightning round of This or That, feeding me such challenging questions as shoes or handbags (shoes), pizza or salad (duh), Jessica Fletcher or Nancy Drew (Nancy. She had the better wardrobe). When we finished, I felt a bit like I'd crossed an active minefield and come out the other side. My one mention of Nick had been when Carl asked me what it was like to join forces with another fashionable resident of the city. I limited my answer to the potential impact such union would have on my closet, and then smiled sweetly. Carl Collins was going to choke on cabbage and there was nothing he could do about it.

We finished and took a short coffee break while the Tradava stock team assembled giant metal racks and hung the samples I'd had delivered. Pam joined me to set up the sunglasses.

"That went well, Samantha," she said. "I knew you had taste and I knew you had style, but I didn't know you could conduct yourself in such a professional manner. I'm beginning to wonder if your talents aren't being wasted in the advertising department."

"Oh, I wouldn't worry too much about that. I'll be plenty busy now that my coworker left."

"All I'm saying is don't be surprised if you hear from me about another job opportunity." She unwrapped the last of the sunglasses, smiled, and rejoined Otto and Harry. The two men waved at me and the three of them left the site.

The photo shoot lasted several hours. The light caught in the windows and shifted, creating glares and highlights on the merchandise I'd set up. More than once I'd had to redo my backdrop. One by one the other people present left the scene, including Carl, who claimed he had to work miracles on our interview to liven it up and deliver on his promise to subscribers of the paper. We finished with the skeleton crew of the photographer, Ragu from Tradava delivery, and me.

At around five, the photographer turned off his camera. "That's a wrap," he said. "Sun's going down and we're getting some weird shadows. If you ask me, you're starting to look a little creepy."

I hadn't asked and was none too happy about having been given the information unsolicited.

"Yeah, I noticed that too," said Ragu. "You look a little pale. Like a vampire or something. Maybe you need more lipstick."

I picked up my coat and held it closed around me. "Or maybe it's the fact that we're inside an empty cement factory and because of the photo shoot I'm not wearing a coat, hat, or gloves and I'm cold?"

The two men looked at each other. "Sure, it could be that," the photographer said. He turned around and left me alone with the merchandise.

Ragu brought the empty cartons from the delivery truck. "You want me to pack up so you can get out of here?"

"No, I'm stuck here until Nick shows up." I pulled out my phone and checked the display. There were no missed calls.

"You didn't get the message?" he asked. "He called the boss. Said he couldn't make it and asked if you'd meet him at his show-room." He picked up a pile of sunglasses and dumped them into a box. "She didn't tell you?"

"No, but she was preoccupied with the Tradava owners." I stared out at the empty street in front of the factory. "I could call a taxi."

"I can give you a ride. Nick's showroom isn't far from Tradava and I have to get the truck back to the store tonight anyway."

"Sure," I said. "Okay," with slightly more conviction. Why would Pam not have given me Nick's message?

We packed up the rest of the merchandise and loaded the van.

Ragu slammed the back doors after the last of the boxes were stacked inside, locked them, and looked at me. "That's everything, right?"

"Right," I said. "Let's get out of here."

I climbed into the passenger side of the Tradava van and Ragu backed up and pulled out of the lot. We drove about half a mile away from the factory when Nick's white truck rounded the corner and passed us going the way we'd come.

29

TOO PANICKED TO THINK STRAIGHT

"Turn around," I said to Ragu.

"What? I can't. This is a two-lane road."

"That was Nick. Turn around at the next turnout and go back. He must be here to get me."

Ragu cursed under his breath but did as I requested. We had to drive farther before the road widened enough for Ragu to safely make the turn. I spent that entire time twisted around in my seat watching the road behind me.

Nick was headed to the factory. But I'd been told to meet him at his showroom. Did that mean somebody wanted to get him away from his showroom? Or they wanted to get him to the factory where I'd been all afternoon? My memory flashed back to the conflicting messages on my first day back at Tradava. Was this what happened the morning Angela was murdered?

All along I'd been thinking that someone wanted to get me to the factory where Vito was, but maybe the goal had been to keep me away from the showroom? If the killer had been with Angela but she thought she had things under control, was it possible she wanted to make sure I didn't get involved?

I glanced at Ragu. He'd been the one to tell me not to wait for

Nick and I was sitting in a van with him. My mind was racing a million miles a minute and I couldn't come up with a single connection between him and Angela di Sotto but I was too panicked to think straight.

"Pull over," I said.

"You wanted me to turn around, now you want me to pull over?"

"Do it. Let me out of the van now."

"We're almost there. Hang on."

"No! Stop the van and let me out or I'm going to jump."

"Carl was right. You're crazy."

He pulled the van over to the side of the road. I unbuckled and jumped out. The van hadn't completely stopped moving and I fell to the ground. My gloved hands took the bulk of the impact and a spear of pain shot through my arm. I screamed. I rolled over onto my back, clutching my left wrist with my right hand. The truck idled a few feet beyond me.

"Kidd?" Nick's voice carried to me.

The Tradava van peeled off around the corner. If I had any lingering concerns about Ragu, his actions didn't exactly assuage them.

Sunset had turned to twilight, and the row of empty factories created long shadows that made it difficult to see. It wouldn't be long before the natural light was completely gone, and we'd be reliant on the occasional streetlamp and headlights from the few cars on the road.

I stood up and hobbled toward the sound of Nick's voice. "Nick?" I called out. "Don't go into the factory!"

Nick met me in the middle of the road. He threw his arm around my shoulders and guided me toward his truck. "Are you hurt?"

"My wrist. It's a long story. Why are you here?"

"To pick you up. Didn't you get my message?"

"The message I got was that you couldn't make it. That I was supposed to meet you at your showroom."

"That wasn't the message. I said I was stuck at my showroom, but I'd be here shortly after five." He guided me to the truck and started the engine. The cab of the truck hadn't had time to cool down and warmth enveloped me.

"Either Ragu misheard the message, or somebody wanted me to think you weren't coming. They wanted to get you here alone or get me to your showroom alone."

"Or both." He looked angry. "I can't be in two places at the same time. If I came here and you went there, they could have gotten to you."

"But now nobody is there."

Nick picked up his phone and hit a recently called number. "Detective, this is Nick Taylor. I have reason to believe something might happen at my showroom tonight. Can you send someone to keep an eye on it?" He paused. "Thank you. I'm at Vito Cantone's factory with Samantha Kidd. Yes. No. Good idea. We're leaving now." He hung up. "Let's get you home." He threw the truck in reverse. It backed up a few feet, and then stalled. He turned the ignition off and then back on. The truck sputtered and then died.

"It sounds like you're out of gas," I said.

"Can't be. I filled up earlier today."

I rolled down my window and looked at the gravel where his truck had been idling. "Um, Nick? Your truck is leaking something." I pointed at the dark, wet stain on the ground.

Nick slammed his fist against the steering wheel. "I hate this!" he said. He pulled his phone back out and stared the display. "Loncar's team is headed to my showroom. What if we're wrong? If I call him back and tell him to come here, what if that's what I'm expected to do?"

"I don't know," I said. "But we're sitting ducks out here," I said. "We should go inside."

I reached for the glove compartment.

Nick put his hand on my wrist and pulled my hand away. "The gun isn't in there," he said.

I squeezed his hand. "Then we'll just have to defend ourselves without it."

In the short amount of time between me jumping out of Ragu's van and Nick helping me to his truck, the sun had completely disappeared behind the horizon and the day had grown dark. The streetlamps had not yet turned on. My guess was that the city's timers were programmed for six or later to conserve electricity. I wished I'd paid more attention to things like that.

I reached out for his arm and winced as pain sliced through my wrist. Nick's expression changed from anger to concern. "You're hurt. How did you hurt yourself?" He pulled off his gloves and gently applied pressure to my wrist with his hands. The cool touch of his fingers felt good around the sprain.

"I jumped out of the Tradava truck while it was still moving. I put my hands out to break my fall."

"Why'd you jump out of the Tradava truck?"

"I freaked out. Ragu told me you left a message with Pam for me to meet you at the showroom, and then I saw your truck. I told him to turn around and bring me back here, but I just kept thinking why would he lie? Why would he tell me that? And I was in his truck completely at his mercy and the thought in my head was to get away from him. I jumped, and he took off."

"Ragu has nothing to do with any of this. He probably went to get help. If he had a connection back to me or to Angela, we would have found it. Besides, I didn't leave a message with Pam. She was busy. I talked to Otto."

"Otto?" I stared at Nick. "As in the owner of Tradava who called in a favor from his friend Vito Cantone so I could use the factory Otto?"

"When you say it like that it doesn't sound so good."

Nausea twisted and knotted my stomach. "Otto told us he knows Vito. He arranged for us to be here today. He heard me tell Pam the cops released your showroom. And he didn't know we were engaged, but Vito did."

"But Otto has nothing to do with my business," Nick said.

"But he might have had something to do with Angela." I closed my eyes. Nick Senior had mentioned the life Angela would have had if she'd grown up in the mafia. Distasteful possibilities ran through my head. A parade of "uncles"—her father's business partners—

around all the time. Vito had told us he kept his relationship to Angela a secret. What if one of those uncles had seen them together and had assumed something completely different?

"The day we first found Angela's body, Loncar told us Angela was Vito's last girlfriend. If that's what the cops who had him under surveillance thought, then it's not a stretch to think other people believed it too."

"You think Otto made a play for Angela."

I got very quiet. "What would Vito do if he found out something like that?"

"Funny you should ask," said a voice outside of my window. It was Otto Tradava. "I've been thinking about that very same question since the day I discovered she was Vito's daughter."

30

FALSE BRAVADO

"Get out of the car," Otto said. He pointed a gun at me, and then at Nick, and then back to me.

I looked at Nick. His hand was still on my wrist. He slid it to my hand and squeezed gently. I squeezed back. Whatever the outcome of tonight would be, we'd go through it together.

Otto walked around to Nick's side of the truck. I opened my door and climbed down. The pulsing pain from my wrist had become a constant, but I blocked it out. I didn't want to give Otto any reason to believe I was hurt.

"Get inside the factory," Otto instructed.

With the gun aimed at close range, I wasn't about to argue. I led the procession into the cavernous structure. I got inside and turned around. Otto stood behind Nick. He stepped closer and pointed the gun at me. "You don't seem scared," he said.

"You're either going to shoot us or not. The choice is yours," I said with false bravado.

I'd had way too many guns pointed at me since my last birthday and I was starting to wonder about this whole older-and-wiser Samantha 2.0 thing. Inside, I was crying, screaming, and bargaining with the powers that be to show me and Nick a way out. I thought the path to maturity would lead to some peace in my life. No dice.

Otto put the muzzle of the gun on the side of my cheek and applied enough pressure to make me turn my head toward Nick. His jaw was clenched, and his body was rigid. Whatever he had in mind, it wasn't just sitting there and watching Otto shoot me. That gave me the tiniest glimmer of hope.

"You went after Angela, but she wasn't interested," I said. The pressure of the gun on my cheek made it difficult to talk.

"I convinced Angela to do some work for me on the side," he said. "Pretty girl. Hard not to notice."

"You didn't know Vito was her father. You made a play for her and she turned you down. But you didn't accept it when she said no, did you?"

"How was I to know? Nobody knew. Vito should have come clean with us. We all thought she was Vito's cupcake. It was a popular opinion. He didn't deserve a woman like her."

"He was her father. They were family," Nick said. "Do you get that? Do you even understand what that means?"

"Sure, I know all about family. I know about my brother Harry inheriting the company and keeping me on with a job title and a yearly stipend one-tenth the size of what the company is worth. How do you think I got involved with Vito in the first place? I'm worth more than what my dad thought when he wrote out his will. My profits from side investments with Vito made up for what I was owed."

"You have quite a way of saying thank you," I said.

"If I'd have known Vito was her dad, I would have backed off," Otto said.

I glanced at Nick. His anger was barely concealed. "But you did know," Nick said. "Maybe not at first, but somewhere along the way, after you crossed the line with her. She said no, and you wouldn't accept that. That's the only reason she'd tell you. It was the one thing she could say that would make you leave her alone. She told you her deepest secret to buy herself some protection and you killed her to save yourself."

"I offered her an alternate career path. She already knew how this life worked. If she joined me, nobody would have touched us. Not even Vito. She should have been grateful, but she wasn't. I had to show her what she was missing out on. She said she would tell Vito what I did if it killed her. Turns out I killed her first."

Nick stepped forward and punched Otto. The knockout was about as expected as the punch Jimmy the Tomato landed on Nick in the parking lot outside of Brother's Pizza. Otto stumbled backward a few steps and waved his hands to regain his balance. The gun went off and a bullet fired into the ceiling.

I grabbed Otto's leg and tried to yank it out from under him. He looked down at me and Nick landed a second punch. Otto fell to the floor. He grabbed my ankle and twisted, and I fell next to him. Something in my left arm snapped on contact with the floor and I screamed with pain. I didn't need to look at it to know it was broken.

Nick rushed to me. He applied gentle pressure around my forearm. I felt tears stream down my face and drip on my light blue suit. "We have to get you to a hospital," he said.

"She won't need a hospital," said Otto from the ground. I looked at him. He still held the gun, this time pointed at me. Slowly he stood up. "Once she's dead she won't feel any pain."

"Samantha's not going to die," Nick said.

"Oh, yes, she is." Otto grinned an eerie grin. "And you're going to be the one to kill her." He waved the gun back and forth between us and stepped forward. Nick had his arm around me and I clutched my broken arm to my body. Pain clouded my thoughts and turned my stomach. Black dots danced in front of my eyes. I felt limp and leaned against Nick for support.

"The way I see it, Mr. Taylor, you've been torn between two women: Angela di Sotto and Samantha Kidd. You killed Angela and now you realize you chose the wrong one."

Nick kept his arm around me. The physical contact let me know he was there, right there. "Nobody will believe I killed Samantha." His voice sounded like it was far away, in a tunnel, or on the other side of the room.

"Nick was here with Vito the day Angela was killed," I said between labored breaths. "*I* found her body."

Otto looked at me. He was quiet for a moment, and through my haze of pain I could tell he was thinking about that one small fact. If Nick had been here with Vito and I'd found Angela's body at Nick's showroom, then how could Otto make people believe Nick was the one to have shot her?

And then the smile returned. "Samantha, you underestimate me. I was here with Vito that morning too. You didn't know that, did you? I knew Nick was on his way. I had it all planned. Confront Nick about his relationship with Angela and tell Vito. Vito would have done the job himself and I would have watched. I would have made a very credible witness."

"Angela knew what you had planned. That's why she told me to get to the factory. She sent me out here to warn Nick. Were you hiding? You probably heard me mention Tradava."

Otto laughed as if we were reliving good times and not the morning he murdered Nick's showroom manager. "I was here when you showed up. When you mentioned Tradava, it was too much of a coincidence. But you being here gave me the perfect opportunity to get to Nick's showroom and take care of Angela. She was no good to me anymore."

Nick's face was red with anger. "Committing murder wasn't enough for you? You had to smash my window and destroy my business?"

"It helped build my case. You killed Angela. Vito found out and retaliated. That's how he does things. Taking Angela's files was the simplest way to send a message that this was about her."

"But you couldn't have done that yourself," I said between labored breaths. "Concrete—too heavy—needed help."

"Help is easy to come by when you're willing to pay. I consider it the cost of doing business." He looked away and stroked his chin. "Maybe I can deduct that on my taxes."

Nick's arm tightened around me and something hard jabbed into my thigh. I'd been holding my broken arm, but I dropped my right hand down into Nick's pocket. My fingers closed around the cold steel of a gun. The gun hadn't been in the glovebox because Nick had already put it in his pocket.

There was no time for questions. I pulled the weapon out and aimed it at Otto. I needed both hands to steady it but even so my fingers didn't want to work.

A shot rang out. Nick shielded me. The gun dropped from my hand. I fell sideways.

Otto crumbled to the ground. A blossom of red spread over the front of his shirt. His feet twitched once, and then he was motionless, his gun still caught in his hand by his side.

Footsteps crossed the catwalk above us. "Move," Nick said. "We have to get out of here."

He pulled me to my feet and I stumbled out of the factory. We were halfway to Nick's truck when a voice spoke behind us.

"Mr. Taylor."

We stopped and turned around. Vito Cantone was framed by the doorway to his factory. The darkness of the interior surrounded him like a shroud. He was dressed in a suit, tie, topcoat. His hands were in his coat pockets. I didn't doubt for a second that one of those pockets held the gun that had shot Otto Tradava.

"I am sorry you were involved in this. Please accept my apologies."

His voice remained so steady that I questioned whether I'd hallucinated the gun shot and the body.

Vito pulled a cell phone out of his pocket and pressed the screen. "Detective Loncar, this is Vito Cantone. There's been a shooting at my factory and I have reason to believe it is related to the murder of my daughter, Angela. The victim is Otto Tradava." He walked toward us, his eyes locked on Nick's face. "Nick Taylor and Samantha Kidd will be able to give you a statement. Ms. Kidd is hurt. She needs medical attention. I'll wait for you here while Mr. Taylor takes her to the hospital." He hung up the phone and gestured toward his town car. "It is better if you go now."

Nick picked me up and carried me to Vito's car, set me on the passenger side seat, and drove away. My last thought was what Loncar would find when he arrived.

31

A FEW DAYS LATER...

*V*ito Cantone was charged with the murder of Otto Tradava, though the case against him was weak. There was a part of me that wanted him to get away with it for Angela's sake. I'd been ready to pull the trigger myself. Angela was Vito's daughter and it was the one action he had left to take on her behalf.

It was the leading story in all the local papers. Carl Collins must have been chaffed that he'd been at the site of the showdown mere hours before it had taken place and still missed the scoop of his life. Despite his due diligence, my profile got bumped. The powers that be at the *Ribbon Times* were confused about how to effectively show-case Tradava the department store without glorifying the store's namesake who had almost killed me. I admit, it was a conundrum.

There was no doubt that Otto Tradava had been shot and killed at Vito's factory. What *was* in question was who had fired the fatal shot. The gun registered to Nick had not discharged. Nor had Vito Cantone's. The gun found at the site that showed evidence of having been fired was the one in Otto's hand. Swabs of his hands and clothing held corresponding gunshot residue that proved he was the one who fired it.

It was my personal belief that Vito had used a secondary

weapon that the police had not found. My curiosity would no doubt return to that question from time to time, though I wondered if I'd ever know the truth.

What I did know was that Otto Tradava had been about to execute either Nick, me, or both of us. He was a desperate madman who feared retribution from the local mafia. He felt shafted by his family when his father left Tradava to his brother and had in turn exerted his power in a series of relationships with women who let him play the role of alpha male until he tired of them. They'd fed his ego in an interchangeable string of romances until he'd set his sights on Angela di Sotto. In his mind, she was one of Vito's cast-off mistresses. His business dealings with Vito had led him to feel entitled to her affections.

Detective Loncar was not happy with the loose ends of the case. He pushed and prodded my statement, looking for something he could use in his greater battle to clean up Ribbon. I told him what I could, but my memories were cloudy, and I could tell he thought I was holding back. Whatever trust we'd established over the past few months had been damaged—perhaps irreversibly.

As for Tradava, I became something of a hero. Ragu had returned to the store and proclaimed me a nut for jumping out of his still-moving van. Stories like that spread through a retail environment like melted mozzarella on breadsticks, and when the story reached Eddie, he'd gone straight to Pam Trotter, who'd called Harry Tradava. Harry knew his brother said he was going back to the factory that night, but he'd expected it to be vacant.

Harry gave the police a statement about his brother's unstable mental condition that backed up everything Vito had said. It made me wonder exactly how long Vito had been standing on the landing above us listening to Otto's rant. I still couldn't decide if he shot Otto to save us or to punish him for what he did to Angela. In a whole lot of ways, I guess it didn't matter. I was alive. Nick was alive. For the moment, life would go on.

Nick carried a tray into my bedroom. It held a bag of pretzels, a bowl of ice cream, and a mug of coffee. No doubt, he knew me, but I was bothered by the fact that I still didn't know him as well as I thought.

"You lied to me," I said quietly. "You said you didn't have the gun."

He set the tray on the corner of the bed. "I said the gun wasn't in the glove box. I'd been carrying it around for days, but I didn't know if I'd have the courage to use it."

"I never thought you'd carry a gun."

"He was going to kill you," he said. "I didn't know what else to do."

It wasn't my place to judge Nick. I'd charged into dangerous situations less prepared than he'd been, but this time—this time I knew he was right. Otto Tradava had meant to kill me and make Nick watch.

"How's the arm?" Nick asked.

"Stiff, but okay." I held up my cast. It fit like a fingerless glove over my hand and ran up to my elbow. I'd opted for black. Too many people had been victims through this and I needed to look at that cast and think about them, not about how my cast would clash with my wardrobe. Samantha 2.0 had developed a little more than I'd anticipated.

Nick pulled back the covers and slid beside me. He bumped his hip against me a couple of times and I scooted aside to make room for him. He put his arm around me and rested against the pillows. "So, this is what your life is like," he said.

"None of it was on purpose," I said.

"I can see that." He kissed the top of my head. "I've been over that night a thousand times and I still don't know what happened."

"Me too."

"But I keep thinking I almost lost you because of my business."

"No. Your business had nothing to do with it. You gave Angela a job for a whole lot of reasons, not the least of which was that she was qualified. You told me yourself she showed up and impressed you with her knowledge and her poise. That was before your dad told you anything about her past."

"If I hadn't given her that job, she might still be alive."

I pushed myself up to a sitting position. "Wow. Okay, I will admit that I come with a certain amount of, shall we say, baggage, but here's the bonus you get for being engaged to me anyway." I took his hand with my good hand. "Angela wanted a normal life. She came to you for a job and during that time, she got what she wanted. She wanted your dad to be her father and she pretended that he was for a long time, but it wasn't until after she felt secure in her identity, after she started working for you, that she acknowledged the truth. Your stability gave her the courage to initiate a relationship with Vito on her terms, as an adult who wanted no part of that life. He respected that. Nobody else in that whole family knew she was his daughter."

"Through everything that happened—the murder, the vandalism at my showroom, your car blowing up, and what happened at the factory—you can still find the bright side?"

I squeezed his hand. "I have to. It's what keeps me going."

Pam Trotter told me to take as much time as I needed before returning to work. Just like returning early the day after my vacation, I had no plans to milk her offer. Tradava's reputation had been hit hard, and rumors circled that the store might not recover. The seventy-five-year-old company was not to be blamed for Otto Tradava's actions. In many ways, his death ensured the company's success. A smart businessman knows how to overcome temporary adversity. A greedy, lazy man will take the easy way every time.

And possibly the most troubling detail of all came to resolution a few days after the news died down. I answered the doorbell and found Jimmy the Tomato on my porch with an insulated carry-out bag.

"I didn't place an order," I said. "Besides, I think it's best if I find another pizza store."

"It's on the house." He undid the Velcro on the side of the bag and pulled out a box. Across the street, I saw the curtains in front of Mrs. Iova's windows move. I waved and smiled. Her curtains dropped back into place.

"Is your fiancé here?" he asked. "I need to talk to you both."

"Follow me." I took the pizza box and walked to the kitchen.

Nick was pouring two glasses of red wine. He looked up. "You have a visitor," I said.

He corked the wine and handed me a glass. I held it but didn't take a sip.

Jimmy slung the empty pizza bag over his shoulder and stuck his hands in the pockets of his loose, faded jeans. "A couple weeks ago, Otto Tradava came into Brothers. He'd been drinking before he got there, and he kept on going. I asked him what was botherin' him and he said you. Said he found out you had a thing going with Angie." Jimmy looked down at the pizza box, and then back up at Nick.

"That's what Otto wanted you to think," I said.

"Vito Cantone is my godfather. Far as I know, I'm the only other person who knew he was her real dad. He asked me to watch out for her because he couldn't."

We stood there in my kitchen, the scent of fresh pizza helping to erase the tension. There was one detail that had bothered me all along, one piece of the puzzle that had been left on the counter after everybody else was satisfied that the picture was complete. "You're the one who called the showroom the morning Angela was murdered."

Nick looked up at me first, and then at Jimmy. We both waited.

"I called Angie every morning. Touch base, make sure nobody was messing with her. You answered the phone and wouldn't put her on, so I knew something was up. Thought maybe you found out too."

"You threatened Nick. You said to tell him to watch his back."

"Yeah. Last thing a guy who's keeping two women wants to hear is that he's being watched. I thought it would scare you off."

"Why'd you punch me?" Nick asked.

"I thought you killed her." Jimmy kept his eyes down on the floor. We all knew he owed Nick an apology. I doubted it was spelled out on the pizza in pepperoni.

"Do you know who smoke bombed my car?"

Jimmy gave me a sideways look. "Heard about that. Kid stuff." he shrugged. "I know a guy who can do the repairs if you want."

"No thanks." Replacing a twenty-year-old car was something I could handle myself.

Logan slinked into the kitchen. He stopped a foot from Jimmy's leg and crouched low. His tail grew fat and he hissed. Jimmy took a step backward like he was scared. The interaction was enough to shake him into action. He looked Nick directly in the eye.

"I'm sorry, man. Vito told me what you and your old man did for Angie." He held out his hand. "We cool?"

Nick shook his hand. "We're cool."

I walked Jimmy to the door and locked it behind him. He was one more man to add to the parade Mrs. Iova saw coming and going from my house, but I didn't care. I went back to the kitchen and found Nick standing in front of the closed box of pizza.

"He didn't offer us a lifetime discount," I said.

"No, he didn't." He flipped the pizza box open. "But he did put on extra oregano."

EPILOGUE

The pizza was a pleasant surprise, as was the rest of the evening. And it turned out I needn't have worried about Nick's sex drive after the case was closed. Once he got a peek at my new leopard printed underwear, all bets were off.

FROM DIANE:

Hello!

After spending time with Samantha as she gets to know Nick's secrets, I can't help wondering about the people we think we know and what happens when we really get to know them. It was in book 5 that Samantha first realized she didn't know Nick as well as she thought. Book 6 when she said yes to his proposal. And here, book 7, where all sorts of issues come to the surface. Personally, I think she handled things in a mature, adult manner. Which may be a poor precedent when Nick's past continues to haunt her in book 8. Oh, wait, I wasn't supposed to mention that just yet.

Samantha may strive to become Samantha 2.0, but as she—and we all—learn, life lessons don't necessarily happen when we plan for them. I hope you'll keep on reading to find out what's next for Samantha, in mystery, in love, and in life.

Xo,
Diane

ABOUT THE AUTHOR

After two decades working for a top luxury retailer, Diane Vallere traded fashion accessories for accessories to murder. She is a national bestselling author and a past president of Sisters in Crime. She started her own detective agency at age ten and has maintained a passion for shoes, clues, and clothes ever since. Sign up for the Weekly DiVa and get girl talk, book talk, and life talk!

Made in the USA
Columbia, SC
08 January 2019